The Necropolis Ghost Train

A Victorian Supernatural Mystery

By

Ken Welch

This book is dedicated to

our grandchildren

Darcy and Nate

"for all the pleasure they have

brought us"

FOREWORD

For many years I have enjoyed reading books to my grandchildren and as they grew older we would often share books or discuss the exciting adventure stories we had read.

The Necropolis railway first captured my attention many years ago and this fascination, together with my grandchildren's shared interest in reading, inspired me to write this book using the railway and cemetery as an atmospheric setting.

Although many people may not be familiar with it, the Necropolis railway actually existed and served London for 87 years transporting bodies and funeral parties from the overpopulated city of London to an overflow cemetery created at Brookwood in Surrey. First opened in 1854, the railway ran regularly until 1941 when the London terminus was badly damaged by a bomb during the Blitz and the railway had to be closed.

Although many aspects of the railway and the locations described in the book are true, other aspects are pure fiction and would not stand close scrutiny should you wish to visit the cemetery which still exists today.

In truth, the combination of ghostly apparitions, foggy cemeteries, dead bodies, steam trains, dark tunnels and wicked crimes was too much for the author to resist and it is hoped that the resulting story will provide sufficient interest to hold the reader's attention and fire the imagination.

Although primarily intended for an age range of 8 to 15, it may also appeal to some of the older generation who still yearn for more simple times when stories were not dictated by modern technology, politics or many of today's more controversial issues.

I very much hope that you enjoy reading it as much as I enjoyed writing it.

Ken Welch

November 2020

Contents

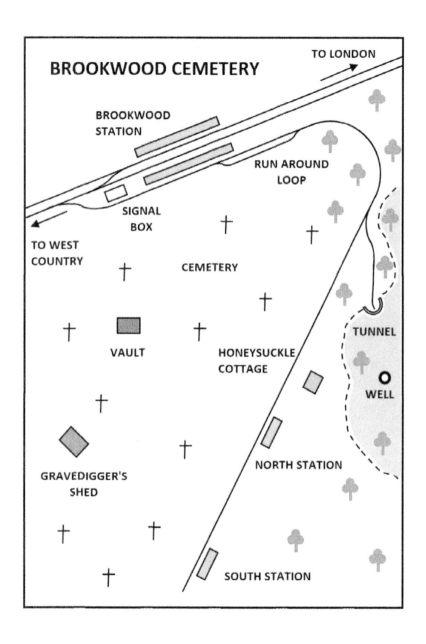

Chapter 1

A Dark Night

Emily wanted to cry. It was dark and it was cold, and now it had started to rain but her mother hurried on through the darkening streets of London with Emily's hand held tightly in her own. "Come along" she said. "We must hurry or we will miss the train."

Emily couldn't remember ever having felt quite so miserable and hugged her doll tightly to her chest with her free hand. They turned a dark corner and Emily almost stumbled on the wet cobblestones but her mother's reassuring hand steadied her. Oh, if only she could climb back into her warm bed. They turned another corner and Emily was thankful to see a row of gas lamps ahead of them, each creating a pool of light in the darkness. The light reflected weakly from the fast forming puddles which were now spreading across the full width of the street, but the alleyways leading off to each side remained dark and ominous. As she hurried past she could hear strange voices drifting out of the darkness, laughing and shouting, but she became really frightened when she heard the sounds of a fight in a side street and the crash of breaking glass.

She had never been to this part of London before but as the thick fog began to drift across the street she could hear the unmistakeable sounds of boats being loaded at the wharves nearby so she realised that they must now be quite near the River Thames. The light from the gas lamps was creating long, frightening shadows on the dark walls that seemed to chase them down the street. She tried to keep her eyes closed but she almost fell again so in a moment of despair she finally said "Can we go home now Mother?"

Mrs Williams stopped and turned to her, and Emily thought she could see tears in her mother's eyes. "No Emily, we won't be going home again."

Mrs Williams looked up again and began to get worried. She had made a wrong turn somewhere and she no longer recognised any of the streets. "Come on", she said, "we must go quickly" and she pulled Emily forwards towards the end of the street where the yellow fog seemed to be lit more brightly by the gas lamps. As they stepped forward they heard a loud noise rushing towards them and Mrs Williams had to pull Emily back against a wall as a large dray horse loomed out of the fog and recklessly thundered past pulling a wagon full of barrels. Mrs Williams smiled at Emily. "That scared me" she said. "We will have to be more careful."

As they moved on, however, it seemed to Emily's relief that the road ahead was now definitely wider and brighter with many more gas lights penetrating the thickening fog. The sounds of more wagons and horses could be heard moving along the road and several passed them with the drivers wrapped up in thick coats and hats pulled down over their faces.

Suddenly Mrs Williams' face lit up as there, slowly making its way along the street, was a cab. "Thank goodness" her mother said, obviously relieved, and she waved the driver down as he approached. He stopped beside them and looked at the pair, clearly concerned.

"You shouldn't be out on a night like this Ma'am, what can I do for you?" he said as he reached down and opened the door for them. Mrs Williams was already pushing Emily onto the step up into the cab and said "Please take us to Waterloo Station" and then paused. "Actually, take us to 121 Westminster Bridge Road please" she said as she climbed into the cab herself.

The driver hesitated and said "But that's the Necropolis Ma'am!" but he was too late as Mrs Williams had closed the door and was getting comfortable in the warm interior. The puzzled driver muttered to himself "It will be closed" but just shrugged and gently tapped the horse with his whip. "Come on Bertie, let's go" and they set off heading for Westminster Bridge which would take them over the river.

Emily was snuggled against her mother, still clutching her doll Elizabeth inside her coat and beginning to fall asleep in the lovely new found warmth. "It's not far so try not to sleep just yet. Once we are on the train you can have a nice long sleep."

It was difficult for her to stay awake, though, and the rhythm of the horse's hooves on the cobblestones together with the rumbling of the wheels was making her feel even more sleepy. She turned to look up at her mother and was about to ask a question when she saw that her mother's eyes were closed. Emily sensed that she wasn't actually asleep but decided not to disturb her. Mother had been upset a lot recently and on several occasions Emily had walked into a room to find her crying, although she had very quickly wiped her eyes and put on a big smile. She snuggled closer to her and, as her eyes closed again, she thought back to when this very strange episode in their lives had all started.

Chapter 2

The Problems

Their "problems" as mother called them had begun about a week ago but the start of the family's changed circumstances had actually begun about three months prior to this. Emily had lived with her mother, father and older sister Kate in a lovely town house in an expensive part of London overlooking Green Park. The family was very well off, Emily's father having made a lot of money mining diamonds in South Africa, and they were fortunate enough to have a several servants to look after them. In truth, Emily didn't see much of her father as he was regularly away for long periods looking after the family's interests in the mine so she had got used to him not being with them at Christmas or missing her birthday parties.

This year, however, how surprised she had been when he arrived home unexpectedly for her 8th birthday. It was such a happy time for them all and instead of sending presents as he usually did, father was able to give Emily her presents in person. One of these was a beautiful china doll which quickly became her favourite and she named her Elizabeth. 'Lizzie' as she called her, went everywhere with Emily and she couldn't bear to be parted from her, even when she went to bed. She became her constant companion and was a very special memory of her father while he wasn't around.

One evening, a week after the birthday party, Mr Williams had sat down with his wife after Emily and Kate had gone to bed and began a serious conversation with her, expressing his concerns over the mining activities in South Africa. He said he had come home to London to speak with their bank manager but would have to return to South Africa soon as he was worried about leaving the running of the mine to his partner, Jack Griffiths, whom he no longer trusted. Strange things had been happening at the mine, unexplained accidents, costly repairs, money going missing and the normally high supply of diamonds being dug out was unusually diminishing. As a result of these losses, Mr Williams had been forced to inject more and more money into the enterprise and had even had to put in money from their own bank account in order to keep the mine working.

He was convinced that his partner was the cause of the problems and was somehow stealing large quantities of the diamonds being dug out and trying to make the mine unprofitable so he could buy it cheaply. Earlier in the year Mr Williams had mentioned to Griffiths that he was thinking of selling his share in the mine so he could spend more time at home with his family and, as a result of this, he now thought that Griffiths was responsible for all the misfortunes at the mine, deliberately making it appear less valuable. He couldn't prove it, however, so he was going back to South Africa to investigate more thoroughly and confront Griffiths. He was so sure of his partner's guilt that, while in London, he had even hired a private detective to look into his background and find out more about him.

Mr Williams then went on to warn his wife that his meeting with the bank manager had not gone well. He had learned that he had put so much money into the mine that their financial position was no longer good and that, unless he resolved the problems soon, the mining company he had created could fail, leading to bankruptcy and possible accusations that Mr Williams had fraudulently taken all the money. If that happened, the shareholders who had invested in the mining enterprise would be very angry and would demand their money back. This revelation had come as a great shock to Mrs Williams but, although she was obviously concerned, she had great faith in her husband and was convinced he would soon sort it out.

Before Mr Williams returned to South Africa he went to visit his brother to explain the situation. His brother, who lived with his mother in a large house in the country near Woking, southwest of London, had been one of the principal investors in the mining company. Uncle John, as Emily knew him, was a kind man but he had never married and spent most of his time working hard as a director of a small railway company. He was a great favourite of hers and she always looked forward to his visits to their house in London.

When Mr Williams explained what was happening at the mine, John was both surprised and concerned but assured his brother that he would do everything he could to look after the family.

"They can always come and live with me if things get really bad" he said but Mr Williams pointed out that the newspaper reporters and stockholders would soon track them down through the family connection and follow them.

"Better that they should go somewhere quiet where they are not known" he said.

John sat back and thought about this, considering the possible options to hide the family. Suddenly his face brightened.

"I know the perfect place" he said "where no-one would ever find them". He seemed very pleased with the idea and that was how they left it.

Two weeks later, Emily's father had said goodbye to the family and set out for the long journey back to South Africa. The voyage had taken three weeks but he wrote to them from ports the ship had stopped at along the way and he wrote to them again as soon as he arrived at the Cape Colony on the southern tip of Africa. His letters arrived regularly after that saying that he had learned a lot about his partner and was hopeful of solving the problems very soon. It was not to be, however, and one night, a few months after he had left London and while

Emily and Kate were asleep in bed, a messenger had called at the London house with a telegram informing them that Mr Williams was missing and was thought to have died when a tunnel he was surveying deep in the mine had unexpectedly collapsed.

Mrs Williams was devastated by the news. At first she refused to believe it but as the reality dawned on her she broke down and cried, spending the rest of the night in tears and in great distress. The servants tried their best to comfort her but it was to no avail as her emotional upset was too great. Her mind was so mixed up with thoughts of her dear husband, how she might never see him again, how life could be so cruel and, of course, how she must now explain this terrible news to Emily and Kate.

Morning came, by which time Mrs Williams was more composed and had resolved to assume that her husband might still be found alive and well. Clutching these thoughts she gave the outward appearance of being calm but was still emotionally distraught inside her head. She managed to put on a brave face when Emily and Kate appeared for breakfast but couldn't bring herself to say anything, deciding to sit down with them later in the morning and explain then. Emily had already sensed there was something wrong. The atmosphere in the house had changed and her mother was being very quiet and evasive. Even the normally friendly servants were behaving strangely, keeping out of the family's way whenever they could and trying not to get drawn into conversation.

Eventually, during their morning tea, Mrs Williams sat down with Kate and asked Emily to come and sit with them. Putting her arm around her, she told them only some of the awful news but emphasised that their father was only missing and that hopefully he would be found soon. The children couldn't take it in at first but as the truth dawned, they both burst into tears which started their mother crying again. The three of them held each other and just sat there in tears, not saying anything more because there was nothing more that could be said.

Kate had been deeply affected by the news and became very depressed so Mrs Williams decided this would be a good time for Kate to visit a distant relative living on the south coast near Lyme Regis. At the age of sixteen, Kate was able to fully understand the seriousness of the situation and the possibility that her father may not be coming back. Mrs Williams thought that some time on her own at the coast might help and give her a distraction so, having made all the arrangements by telegram, Kate and Maria, one of the servants, were packed off in a horse drawn carriage. Emily was sorry to see her go as, despite their age difference, they were very close and Kate always looked after her like a second mother.

Chapter 3

Time to Leave

A few days later the story of Mr Williams' disappearance broke in one of the London newspapers. The bold headlines made all sorts of wild accusations including claims that the mining company had been bankrupt for some time and that Mr Williams had run away with all the money or that, filled with guilt, he had even killed himself which caused a lot of upset in the Williams household. In no time at all a large crowd formed outside the house, initially made up of mostly newspaper journalists but these were quickly joined by unhappy investors demanding the return of their money. The house was besieged and it was no longer safe to leave although the servants were still able to use the back entrance which led out onto a quiet alleyway.

It wasn't long before there was a visit from the family's bank manager who advised Mrs Williams that, before his distressing disappearance, her husband had sent several messages from South Africa to draw out all of the remaining mining company funds and all of the Williams family's personal money to be transferred to him as soon as possible. The money was duly sent but had now strangely disappeared, having been withdrawn from the South African bank shortly after it had arrived. As a result, the bank manager now regretted having to advise Mrs Williams that she no longer had any money left in the bank and she was now virtually penniless.

As he drank tea brought in by the maid, he apologised adding that he didn't have any other information that he could give her at this time and admitted that he had been quite baffled by the very odd turn of events.

"Your husband is a sensible man" he said "and it is quite unlike him to do anything so rash. I am in contact with the manager of the bank in South Africa and he is looking into it for me to try to find out where all that money went."

When he had left the house a short while later he had great difficulty walking back to his cab which had been patiently waiting at the kerb. The crowd had become much larger and noisier during the morning and as he crossed the pavement he had been bombarded with questions and even jostled by a few of the more belligerent people in the angry gathering.

Mrs Williams was stunned by this latest revelation about their finances and was sitting quietly in the drawing room after lunch considering the situation and its implications on their future lives when there was a sudden loud crash as a brick was thrown through the window and fragments of glass flew across the floor. She covered her face in shock but, quickly recovering, she leapt out of her chair and rushed out of the room. It had been lucky that Emily hadn't been playing on the floor at the time and was upstairs in the nursery. The servants had quickly cleared up the mess but this sudden act of violence had left Mrs Williams now feeling very frightened.

Later that afternoon another visitor arrived. It was Uncle John who, without waiting to be announced by the housekeeper, rushed into the room obviously out of breath and looking very flustered.

"I'm so sorry I couldn't get here any sooner" he said as he gave Mrs Williams a gentle hug and kissed her cheek. "I've been in the north of England all week on business but travelled back as soon as I got your telegram."

Mrs Williams asked him to sit down and told him the full story but admitted that she didn't fully understand the situation yet and was completely mystified by the latest developments. The shouting from the street had become louder during their conversation and Emily had wandered into the room, worried by the noise. Her face brightened when she saw her uncle and she rushed forward and climbed onto his knee.

"I hear you're being a brave girl" he said. He pointed to her doll, Lizzie, and said "has she been behaving herself" and continued to engage her in casual conversation simply to take Emily's mind off what was happening outside.

Emily spent some time telling him what she and Lizzie had been doing but she eventually settled down and began to play with her doll on the floor as her uncle turned back to Mrs Williams.

"There isn't much time" he said. "I am on my way to the station now to get a train to Southampton and I have booked passage on the fast steamship *SS Britannia* to the Cape Colony. I have had some telegrams with additional information from an old friend out there but I still don't know what is really happening at the mine and I need to get out there as quickly as possible to investigate. It all sounds very suspicious and I'm determined to find out the truth."

He paused and then, after checking that Emily was not within earshot, he said quietly "You have to leave here tonight. I will speak to the Police Commissioner whom I know quite well and ask him to send an officer to try and disperse the crowd outside. He will also need to guard the outside as the house isn't safe any longer. I have already made some arrangements for you to move but I will have to bring the plan forward now as it's far too dangerous for you to stay here."

Mrs Williams was taken aback but he insisted she had no choice, if only for the safety of the children. He then told her to pack a small bag and gave her instructions on what to do. As he was leaving he said she was not to worry and he would get to the bottom of this and he would send her a message as soon as he could

Chapter 4

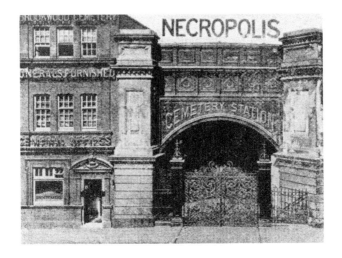

Necropolis Station

Emily was still in a deep sleep as the cab continued on its way to the station. She was dreaming and, as in her previous dreams, she could hear faint voices whispering in the background but couldn't quite make out what they were saying. She had often had strange dreams which had worried her family but Emily had eventually got used to them and didn't feel threatened by them anymore. There was a sudden bump as one of the wheels went into a large hole in the road and the sharp jerk made her jump and immediately wake up. She looked out of the window and could see that they were crossing a bridge. The darkness and the fog, which was still thick, prevented her from seeing much of the river below but as she stared, she occasionally had brief glimpses of the water reflecting the yellow light from the gas lamps on the riverside and from the lanterns on the barges drifting under the bridge.

The bridge was soon lost in the swirling fog and rapidly left behind them as the cab continued on its lonely way, only occasionally meeting vehicles passing in the opposite direction. Emily was no longer tired and she realised that her weariness had now passed and she was feeling very alert. This was actually beginning to be something of an adventure and she recalled her mother saying that they were going on a train. Emily had never been on a train before and the prospect was very exciting.

The cab turned left round a sharp corner and the driver brought the horse to a stop outside a tall old building. There were two large iron gates set into the wall and one of them was open, leading into a dark entranceway which was wide enough to take wagons and carriages. "We're here Ma'am", said the driver opening the door. "You're in luck, it looks as if the station is open after all."

She paid the driver and thanked him. He smiled and nodded to Emily and tipped his hat to Mrs Williams.

"Have a safe journey" he said and with a friendly "Come on Bertie" the horse set off again and soon disappeared into the fog.

It was suddenly very quiet and Emily felt cold again as she hugged Lizzie to her chest. She looked up and at the top of the building she could see a large sign that said *NECROPOLIS*. There was also a small door at ground level which had a sign saying *General Offices* but Mrs Williams took Emily's hand and, remembering her instructions, walked instead through the adjacent open gate into the dark entrance. Ahead of them the roadway stretched about 20 yards and suddenly turned sharp left before going quite steeply uphill. Just on the corner, however, there was a small office on the right with a bright light showing through a small window. There was a door alongside and, in the light reflected from the window, Mrs Williams saw a board on the door which read *Stationmaster*. She politely knocked and walked in, pulling Emily behind her.

They entered a small room, brightly lit by two gas lamps on the far wall overhanging an old, polished wooden desk and chair. Next to it was an equally old bookcase which, like the desk, was untidily covered in files and papers. The most inviting feature, however, was a blazing fire at the far end of the room over which a kindly looking man in shirtsleeves and waistcoat was bent, prodding the fire with a poker and causing clouds of sparks to fly up the chimney. Emily noticed that a good few of the sparks flew out of the fire onto what looked like a frequently singed rug.

The kindly looking man turned as they walked in and stood up.
"Ah, you must be Mrs Williams" he said with a huge smile on his face. He reached for his stationmaster jacket and quickly slipped it on over his shirt.
"Sorry for my appearance. I've been expecting you but what a terrible night for you to be out. Please come over here by the fire and get yourselves warm while I make you some tea".

Mrs Williams gratefully walked over to the fire and she and Emily sat in two comfortable armchairs on each side of the fire. Emily immediately felt the heat from the fire on her face and hands warming her up and thought to herself that she had never been in such a cosy room.

"You must be Mr Dawkins" Mrs Williams said as he lifted the kettle off a small range above the fire. "I'm so sorry that we are late but I lost my way in the fog".

As Mr Dawkins busied himself making the tea he said "Oh don't worry about that. I must admit that I was getting concerned that you weren't coming but there's really no rush as the train won't leave until I let it. Plenty of time for your tea. And what would you like to drink young lady?"

Emily looked at her mother, unsure of what she should say but he added "I have some milk here and I could warm that up for you if you would like it?"

Mrs Williams smiled and Emily politely said "Thank you Mr Dawkins, that would be lovely".

As they sipped their hot drinks, he pulled up another chair next to Mrs Williams and quietly spoke to her. He said that Director Williams had briefly called in on his way to Southampton and fully explained the situation to him so Mr Dawkins, as stationmaster, had been able to make all the necessary arrangements for their trip that night. He also confided that he now felt a personal responsibility for them and if they ever needed any help, Mrs Williams was to contact him immediately. She felt very reassured by this kindly man and thanked him again.

He turned to Emily who had only been half listening to the conversation.

"Are you looking forward to the train ride" he said.

Emily gave a big smile and nodded. "I've never been on a train before" she informed him.

"Well", he said "you're in for a big treat. Not many people get to ride on a special train like this one, and we never usually have passengers at night".

He turned back to Mrs Williams and, lowering his voice again said "Unfortunately there wasn't much time with the short notice I had and the train crew tonight are a miserable bunch but you won't see much of them and they don't know the full story about8 you. In any case, Mrs Robinson will get in touch with you tomorrow to help you settle in so you are not to worry about finding your way around".

Mrs Williams smiled again as they finished their drinks. "Thank you, you have been most kind".

Mr Dawkins pulled a large watch out of his waistcoat pocket and looked at the time. He checked it against a large clock hanging over his desk and said "I think we should be getting you on the train now. I'll show you the way up to the platform".

He reached down and took Mrs Williams' bag and stepped back to allow his visitors to walk out of the office first. He then led them up the sloping roadway which soon turned right and continued up into the gloom beyond. After the bright lights of the office, it seemed very cold and damp again and the fog was drifting down the ramp towards them.

"I'm sorry about the long walk" said Mr Dawkins. "This roadway has to be wide to allow the carriages and wagons to get up to the platform level but they usually only come during the day so, with the glass roof, we don't need a lot of light. We also had a lift installed recently which is another way to get the coffins up to the platform".

Emily tucked Lizzie carefully inside her coat and held her mother's hand tightly as they walked.

Mr Dawkins went on "The trains and platform are a lot higher than the road outside so the ramp has to be fairly steep which can be difficult in the icy weather". They soon reached the top of the slope which led onto two wide platforms with two railway tracks coming in between them. On one of these tracks, a line of carriages waited with the engine at the far end of the platform, standing on its own, almost lost in clouds of steam and smoke which added to the thickening fog. A loud hissing noise could be heard coming from the engine with occasional blasts of steam, all of which sounded quite frightening to Emily.

The guard of the train was fixing a red lamp to the back of the last carriage and turned as they approached.

"Good evening Mr Dawkins" he said. "I'm guessing these will be our unscheduled passengers".

"That's right Mr Parker, and you are to ensure that they get to Brookwood safely if you please".

The guard looked down at his feet. "Mmm, Sykes isn't very happy about it. We're not supposed to have passengers on the night runs".

"Well I don't care what driver Sykes thinks. This is a special request from the Director and if Sykes knows what's good for him he'll do what he's told".

That was clearly an end to the conversation and the guard turned to busy himself with the lamp again. Mr Dawkins had little patience with Sykes who could be very difficult at times but he was a good train driver and knew a lot about engines. His sour nature made him few friends but he seemed to get on well with his fireman, William O'Hare, whom Mr Dawkins thought was a very devious character and very untrustworthy.

Mr Dawkins led Mrs Williams and Emily to the front of the train and opened one of the carriage doors.

"This our best, first class carriage" he said proudly. "The lamps are already lit and you should be very comfortable in here".

They stepped in and settled down on the comfortable seats while Mr Dawkins put their bag on the luggage rack.

"There" he said, and he stepped down from the carriage back onto the platform. "I have to go and talk to the guard now but don't you forget, if you have any problems or if there is anything I can ever do for you, just send me a message here at the station."

"Thank you Mr Dawkins" Mrs Williams said. "I so much appreciate everything you have done for us and I will make sure the directors hear of it".

Mr Dawkins smiled, nodded as he lifted his hat and gave Emily a wink as he closed the door, before turning and walking back down the platform.

Chapter 5

Night Train

Emily couldn't contain her excitement as she looked around the carriage compartment, all thoughts of being tired having now left her. The seats were soft and she could bounce on them, the walls were wood panelled with pictures of restful mountain scenes, and the whole compartment was bathed in the warm light from four lamps.

"Is this all for us?" she said.

"Yes Emily, all for us so just settle down now".

Emily didn't want to settle down though. "Will we go really fast and see things rushing past the window" she said.

"Only if the fog is not too thick" Mrs Williams replied laughing "but it may be better once we get out of London into the countryside." She put her arm around Emily and they finally began to relax after their busy evening.

They sat quietly, waiting in anticipation but after just a few minutes, the rather loud hissing noise coming from the locomotive at the end of the platform abruptly stopped and there was a short blast from the engine's whistle followed by a puffing noise as it slowly reversed back towards the carriages. The puffing noise stopped and Emily listened to the sounds of the engine's wheels getting closer as the engine rolled along the railway track towards them. Suddenly there was a loud squeal as the brakes were applied and the carriage jerked as the engine gently bumped into it and stopped. As she listened she could hear the sounds of men talking and heavy metal links being hooked on as the engine was coupled to the carriages.

Although Emily couldn't see it from inside the carriage, the signal at the end of the platform had now changed to *CLEAR* and the guard at the back of the train blew his whistle and waved a green flag before climbing into the last carriage. Driver Sykes had been leaning out of his cab window watching the guard and as soon as he saw the flag he stepped back inside, gave a quick blast on the train whistle, let off the brake and gently opened the regulator. Emily heard a loud burst of steam and felt a strange sensation as the train slowly but gently began to move forward. This was really exciting and she gripped the armrest to steady herself.

The engine began to puff, slowly at first but more rapidly as the train began to pick up speed. The carriage rocked from side to side and now she could see the station walls and the platform lamps sliding past the window though it all seemed so unreal, as if she were stationary and the outside world was moving. The movement was getting faster and faster until, suddenly, the outside went very dark as the platform and buildings were left behind and she found herself looking at nothing but swirling smoke and fog. She strained to see more and, as her eyes got used to the darkness, small points of light began to appear in the distance, a few at first and then more and more.

The train was going quite fast now and the wheels were making a regular clickety-clack sound as they sped over the rails. There was less rocking in the compartment too and Emily was brave enough to stand up and put her face against the window to get a better view. The fog momentarily lifted and there were the lights again, spread out like a huge blanket stretching into the distance and she realised that she was now looking across the dimly lit houses of London. It was such a beautiful sight, the lights twinkling in the night and even reflecting off the nearby River Thames, the darkness, smoke and fog working together to hide the true dirt and grime of the city. The fog then descended more thickly than before and the beautiful vision was lost again.

"I think you should sit down now Emily" Mrs Williams said. "I don't think you will see much for the rest of the journey."
Emily returned to her seat, disappointed that the fog was so thick. She sat, but continued to look out the window, hoping to see more. Her thoughts were still very mixed up but she slowly came to realise that her excitement was wearing off and being replaced by curiosity. She plucked up her courage.
"Will you tell me where we are going, Mother?" she asked.

Before Mrs Williams could reply, the train gave a long whistle and they both jumped as they saw lights flashing past the window and heard a loud rushing noise as the train thundered through a deserted station. Emily just managed to read the name *VAUXHALL* on a large sign on the platform before the train noisily left the station behind and rushed on into the darkness. She also became aware of an awful smell drifting into the carriage and wrinkled her nose in disgust.

"Well, I wouldn't like to live here, Emily" laughed Mrs Williams. "That's the smell of the London gasworks". She moved across to sit on Emily's side of the compartment and put her arm around her.

"Yes, it's time I told you where we are going to live."

"We are on our way to a place in the country called Brookwood. It's not too far from London and will only take about fifty minutes to get there by this train. Uncle John knew of a small cottage there that was empty and would suit us perfectly. You see, we need to be somewhere quiet for a time, to get away from the nasty crowds that you saw outside our old house, the newspaper journalists and all the people who are upset about losing their money. They can be very unkind so we are going to a secret place where they won't find us until this is all sorted out. That was why we left home when it was dark and why we went out of the servants' back door."

Emily thought about this for a moment. Her mind was still in a turmoil but moving to the country didn't sound too bad she thought and then she asked "Will the cottage have a garden?"

"Well, sort of" said Mrs Williams. "In fact this is going to sound a little strange but the cottage is situated in a very large remembrance garden. What that means is that we are going to live on the edge of a cemetery".

She paused to let this sink in, knowing full well what the next question would be. Emily knew what a cemetery was and she wasn't happy at this startling piece of news. "Will there be people buried in the garden then?"

After a brief pause she continued, her eyes suddenly becoming wide. "Will there be ghosts Mother?"

Mrs Williams gave her a hug and said soothingly "No Emily, there are no ghosts as I have told you before so you must not worry" but Emily didn't feel reassured.

Ever since she could remember Emily had suffered from strange dreams which had been a constant source of worry for her parents. Sometimes, when she looked out onto the street at night, Emily had seen strange figures just standing or drifting slowly across the road into the park. Despite having normal faces, the figures didn't seem like real people somehow as they were very indistinct and stayed in the shadows but they were always dressed in white. Her mother had tried to make light of it but in her conversations with her husband she confessed that Emily's grandmother had been born with the same condition and was well known in the family for seeing strange things and even predicting the future. Mr Williams just said that he had no time for fortune tellers and told his wife that Emily would simply grow out of it in time. Mrs Williams knew she wouldn't, however, and was always very conscious of Emily's dreams and the voices she heard, and would regularly worry about how it might affect her.

Emily was still staring out of the window at the fog swirling past the carriage.

"Let me explain what the cemetery is for" said Mrs Williams. "London is a very big city and it is getting more and more overcrowded every year. Sadly, with the poor conditions in London, there are a lot of deaths. I'm sure you will understand that when people die from old age, disease or accidents it is usual for them to be buried in the city graveyards and cemeteries but these have been getting full for a long time and a new burial place was needed. Brookwood is a huge open space that has been turned into an overflow cemetery to take many of the burials away from London. There are lots of families and mourners travelling from London to Brookwood cemetery every day with the bodies of their departed loved ones and this railway has been specifically built to provide the means to transport them. It's called the *London Necropolis Railway*.

Mrs Williams went on. "Your Uncle John is a Director of the railway company so he has a very important position and that was how he arranged for us to go into hiding in a cottage down there. The cemetery is so big, it actually has two stations for the different types of passenger. There is a stationmaster, Mr Roberts, who apparently looks after both stations and although the cottage was originally built for him, he doesn't use it as he prefers to stay in his own house with his wife and children in the nearby village of Brookwood. In fact, we will be getting to know his wife, Mrs Roberts, very well as she has offered to help us by working as our housekeeper."

Just then the train thundered through another station, larger than the last one with more lights and Emily was momentarily distracted, briefly glimpsing a sign saying *CLAPHAM JUNCTION* before she turned back to her mother.

"Are there bodies on this train?" she asked. There was a pause.

"Yes Emily" said her mother. "There are some different carriages called Hearse Carriages in the train which carry the coffins but they never let people travel in the same carriage with them."

Mrs Williams thought she had said enough and remained silent as Emily absorbed what she had been told. It was all so very strange. There had been excitement in her mind, yes, but now it was very worrying and thoughts of ghosts and bodies still terrified her. The train thundered on as she thought everything over.   There was still nothing to see outside so she thought the fog must be very thick now although sometimes clouds of smoke from the engine could be seen rushing past, lit up by the light from their compartment. With thoughts of ghosts still dominating her thoughts, the swirling smoke and fog outside took on strange forms which danced around the window and seemed to be chasing the train. Was she imagining it or were those shapes following them?

"This train" she thought, "…. is a *Ghost Train*".

As she stared at the fog, the shapes which had reflected the white carriage lights continued to chase them for some time but eventually seemed to fade and, to her relief, slowly disappeared.   Very soon the rhythmic clickety-clack of the wheels on the railway track became quite sleep-inducing, making her feel tired again. She looked up at her mother and could see that her eyes were now closed. She snuggled down again and in no time at all, Emily was asleep too.

Chapter 6

A Strange Arrival

Emily didn't know how long she slept but a sudden whoosh and blast of air violently shook their carriage and they both woke up to see the lights of another train rushing past them in the other direction, heading towards London. In just a few seconds it was past them and lost again in the darkness but they could now feel that their own train was slowing down, the noise of the wheels and the rapid puffing from the engine now getting slower and slower. There was a long whistle and the train slowly pulled in to a well-lit station and finally came to a standstill.

"I think we have arrived" said Mrs Williams. "Can you see the name of the station?"

Emily peered out of the window and further down the platform she could see a sign.

"Yes Mother, it says *BROOKWOOD*. Do we get out now?"

"No" Mrs Williams said. "Apparently we have to stay on the train while it reverses off the main line into the cemetery."

The train stood waiting for several minutes without anything happening but then, over the hissing noise coming from the engine, they could faintly hear the sounds of raised voices outside on the platform as if there was an argument taking place. Although they couldn't hear what was being said, a few words could just be made out.

"No, it's too risky tonight … we can't do it with strangers about"

"Foxy needs them so there's no choice "

"We'll have to go in engine first"

Mrs Williams frowned wondering if she and Emily were the "strangers" being talked about but suddenly a face appeared at the window and, judging by his coat and cap, Mrs Williams guessed it was driver Sykes. Without any apology he opened the door and stepped inside.

"It will be dark on the journey through the cemetery and there will be nothing to see so you should keep the window blinds down" he said in a very abrupt manner. "You shouldn't look out as it can be very scary at night and there are stories of strange goings on in the dark".

Emily's eyes went wide at this but without another word Sykes pulled down the blinds and, after furtively looking down the platform, he stepped out and closed the door behind him.

Mrs Williams was taken aback but, recovering from the somewhat surprising interruption, she smiled and said "Well that was interesting, wasn't it". She took Emily's hand and added "There's nothing for you to worry about my dear."

More angry voices were heard from the platform outside.

"Sykes, get that train off the main line immediately. The night mail express is due in ten minutes."

There was a sudden increase in the hissing coming from the engine and after a short blast on the whistle Emily felt the train begin to slowly move forward again. It didn't pick up speed, however, and after a short distance once again came to a standstill. As was usual, the train had been pulled clear of the platform and the signalman in the station signal box had switched the points behind it to allow it to reverse back into the cemetery on the private line. Emily felt the train moving backwards, swaying from side to side as it rattled very slowly over the points and continued further into the cemetery.

It soon came to a standstill again, still close to the station, and there were sounds of the engine being uncoupled from the carriages. Emily was confused and asked "Should we get out here then Mother?"

"No darling, Uncle John explained that there would be a delay here. For safety reasons they have to move the engine around to the other end of the train so it can pull the carriages through the cemetery instead of pushing them backwards. There is a special loop in the railway track here with things they call points at each end to allow them to run the engine around".

As she spoke, the engine rolled past on a parallel track and a few minutes later there was a slight bump as it was re-connected to the opposite end of the train and began to pull the carriages further into the cemetery.

Suddenly Emily heard an eerie shriek in the distance. It was a wild, frightening sound which was rapidly getting louder as it approached them. Emily was frozen to her seat, afraid to move. It sounded unearthly and was surely a ghost from the cemetery coming to get them. The noise continued to grow, ever closer but she was too afraid to even reach out to her mother. Her worst fears about ghosts were coming true. Then, just as all seemed lost, she heard the unmistakable sounds of a steam train and realised it was the continuous whistle of a fast express on the main line. The noise had risen to an ear splitting scream as the night mail thundered through the station and on into the darkness, making its non-stop run to the West Country. Emily's mother laughed and said "Well, I'm glad they moved our train when they did".

Their own train continued its slow way through the cemetery but it suddenly lurched to one side, clattering over the tracks and very quickly the sounds of the engine became strangely louder, yet muffled and echoing. The train stopped again and there were the sounds of feet running past the carriage and a voice whispered "Hurry". It seemed very strange but became even stranger when some doors were heard to open followed by some muffled banging and scraping. A voice whispered more urgently "For goodness sake be quiet".

Mrs Williams was confused as Uncle John hadn't mentioned this. What on earth was going on? Emily wished the blinds weren't down so she could see out, despite the warnings of scary things happening in the cemetery. She bravely lifted the blind slightly and cautiously peered into the night but was surprised at what she saw. There appeared to be no fog outside now and the night was totally black except for two partially darkened lanterns further down the track. By their faint glow she could vaguely see rough, dark walls and three figures working alongside the track, bent over as they moved some large boxes. One of them suddenly looked up and, raising one of the lanterns, he cautiously looked back along the train. She quickly let the blind drop down again and sat back in her seat, feeling guilty. She wondered what was going on and was about to tell her mother what she had seen when the train started moving backwards again until after a short distance it stopped, before changing direction once more and moving forward. It was all very strange.

After a few more minutes of slowly rolling through the cemetery the train once again came to a standstill, this time accompanied by a very loud hissing noise from the engine as if it were exhausted by its night's work. There was a sharp knock on the door and it was opened by the guard, Mr Parker. He looked a little subdued and didn't look them in the eye as he said "This is where you get out Ma'am".

Mrs Williams collected her bag and helped Emily to step out onto the platform which was quite well lit by several gas lamps, despite the all-pervading fog which now seemed just as thick as it had been in London. It drifted across the lamps, creating an eerie, almost frightening picture. After the warm carriage, the outside air seemed very cold and Mrs Williams bent down and wrapped her shawl around Emily to keep her warm. As she took in the scene, Emily noticed that two men, presumably Driver Sykes and the Fireman, had opened some carriage doors further down the train and were already unloading some rather familiar-looking large boxes onto the platform.

Mr Parker pointed towards the end of the platform and, in the far distance, they could just make out through the fog some lights shining through the windows of a small building.

"That's where you'll be staying. There's a sort of pathway at the end of the platform and the cottage door isn't locked. I've to tell you that Mrs Robinson left the lights on for you with a meal on the stove and she will call in to see you tomorrow to make sure you're settled in properly. Now, if you'll excuse me, we have to turn the train round and take it back to London to get it ready for the morning run". With that, he turned and walked down the platform to join the others.

Chapter 7

A New Home

Emily woke up in a warm bed and looked around at her new room. She had not been able to see it properly when she went to bed in the dark last night and, being so tired from her exhausting day, she had fallen asleep very quickly although her mother had stayed with her until she was sure she was sleeping soundly.

The walk through the fog to their cottage had been difficult and would have been helped enormously if the train crew had provided them with a lantern. It was quite scary in the dark and Emily held her mother's hand very tightly. She was convinced they were being followed and kept looking over her shoulder. The fog swirled about them creating strange shapes which were frightening enough but at one point she saw something that terrified her. In the distance, standing between two gravestones, she could see what appeared to be a small white figure. Its shape was indistinct and its outline seemed to be constantly changing, like the drifting fog around it, but she was sure it was the figure of a person, just standing and staring. She had quickly looked away and closed her eyes as she squeezed closer to her mother.

They eventually reached the door of the cottage and walked in. It was a lovely sight, well lit, with comfortable seats, heavy curtains and a warm fire. On the stove was a large pot of stew giving off a delicious smell while a fresh loaf and butter were waiting on the table. All thoughts of the white figure were quickly dispelled. They decided to explore the cottage later and, after warming themselves by the fire, they settled down to their meal. As they sat at the table, they heard the train rumble past on the nearby track on its way back to Brookwood station where it would re-join the main line to London. Thoughts of trains were no longer of interest, however, as they enjoyed their meal.

"This is delicious" said Mrs Williams. "Do you think we could persuade Mrs Robinson to come and cook for us every day?" Emily just laughed and ate some more stew before they decided it was time for bed.

Today was a new day, however, and as she climbed out of her comfortable bed Emily felt very excited. There was the cottage to explore, and perhaps a garden she could play in, but she wasn't so sure about the cemetery beyond and shuddered at the thought of seeing it. She placed Lizzie on her pillow and, after walking to the window, very carefully opened the curtains a little so she could look out.

What a sight met her eyes - it took several minutes to take it all in. The fog had gone and it was a bright day, the sun shining in a clear blue sky. Close to the ground a mist had formed, several feet thick, like a sea of grey slowly drifting past and stretching as far as the eye could see, while rising up out of the mist were gravestones and monuments of different types and sizes, many in the shape of tall crosses while others were like small church spires or figures like angels. Further to the right there was an area of high ground and the mist was pouring down the slope like some kind of waterfall. Unlike London, there wasn't a soul in sight and the only sound was of birds singing. It was a totally unexpected, almost magical picture and all thoughts of fearful graves, dead bodies and mysterious white shapes were driven from her mind. Emily got dressed and rushed downstairs where her mother was already preparing breakfast with more things that Mrs Robinson had left in the larder including some homemade jam and a jar of honey. She ate as quickly as was polite, telling her mother between mouthfuls about the wonderful view from her bedroom window while all the time being anxious to leave the table and explore.

When they had finished, they decided to look at the rest of the cottage. They had already used the kitchen and dining area which was just alongside the front door entrance but on the other side of the hallway was a door leading to a cosy parlour where you could sit on comfortable seats by a big open fire. There was a table to work on and a large window protruding from the front of the cottage providing lovely views to either side. A window seat was positioned in the window recess and Emily quickly decided that this would be her favourite place to sit and read or perhaps play with Lizzie while enjoying the view. There was also a small room at the back of the house that was a bit dusty and looked unused except for storing odds and ends. Upstairs, of course, there were the two bedrooms, the large one which had been used by Mrs Williams and the slightly smaller one with two beds which Emily would share with Kate when she finally arrived.

While they were tidying the bedrooms, there was a knock at the door and Mrs Williams went downstairs to see who had called. Emily was more interested in looking in all the cupboards and drawers of her room but, having found them all empty, she went downstairs to see who had arrived. Mother was sitting in the parlour with a kindly looking lady who smiled at Emily as she entered the room. Emily instantly decided she liked her. "Come in" said her mother. "This is Mrs Robinson who kindly left the lovely meal for us last night".

Mrs Robinson had come to check that they had found everything to their liking and said that, although very busy, she would be very happy to come to the cottage if they needed any help, to tidy, do the washing or prepare meals for them. She explained that she would be around every day as she worked there in the cemetery. There were two stations in the cemetery grounds and not only did she clean and tidy them, she also managed the refreshment rooms on the station platforms. Funeral parties arrived every day and the railway company thought it appropriate that the mourners should be able to obtain refreshments after the funerals, before their journey back to London.

"It's a full time job looking after two stations" she said "and I keep telling my husband, George, that I need help but he's always too busy to do anything about it."

George Robinson was the stationmaster and his day was fully occupied with a variety of jobs. His primary role was in ensuring the timely flow of trains and the burial service arrangements at the cemetery stations but he was also responsible for managing the grave digging, the maintenance of the cemetery and sometimes alternating with another stationmaster to look after the Brookwood mainline station.

"Anyway" said Madge "don't you worry about me being busy Mrs Williams as I can always fit your little jobs in. This is a lovely little cottage and it will be easy to look after, and I don't think you will be needing me to come in every day anyway."

Emily soon realised that Mrs Robinson talked a lot and she was desperate to ask a question so when she paused for breath Emily quickly asked "Why do you need two stations Mrs Robinson?"

"Why bless you dear" she said "why don't you call me Madge. I like to be called Madge".

She went on "We have to keep the mourners apart because they follow different religions and they each have their own funeral arrangements and customs so they are best dealt with in a respectful manner with some at the North Station and the others at the South Station. They have their own priests and ceremonies too and it's all lovely for them but of course we have to remember that it's also a very sad occasion for them".

Madge went on to explain that she had two sons, one about Emily's age while the other was now seventeen years old and worked on the trains as a fireman.

"He does the funeral run from London most days so you will see him around quite a lot. He stays in London during the week with his driver friend but often comes home to stay at weekends."

Just as Mrs Williams was thinking that she was going to talk all morning, Madge looked at the clock on the wall and jumped up saying "Goodness me, is that the time! I should have been cleaning the station waiting rooms and getting the refreshment rooms ready by now. The first train is due at 11 o clock." With that she apologised for having to rush off but said she would call back after lunch to sort out the cleaning arrangements for the cottage.

Mrs Williams drew her to one side on her way out and said quietly "Madge, this is a bit embarrassing but, well, I can't afford to pay much."

Madge gave her one of her big smiles and simply said "Oh, don't you fret about that my dear, we are all friends down here and I'm sure we can sort something out until you get back on your feet again."

With that, and after patting Emily on the head, she hurried out of the door. Emily watched as she rushed down the path, the ground mist swirling around her dress as she went. Mrs Williams smiled as she turned to Emily. "Well, what do you think of Madge then?" she said with a twinkle in her eye.

"I thought she was lovely" said Emily to which her mother replied "So do I. I think we are going to be very happy here".

Chapter 8

Exploring the Cemetery

Later that morning Mrs Williams sat Emily down and explained to her that, while staying at Brookwood, she would not be going to the local school but would be taught at home.

"We will have lessons in the morning but then you can take the afternoon off to play and amuse yourself. We won't start just yet though as it will take a while for us to settle in."

To Emily's great joy, Mrs Williams then asked if she would mind amusing herself for a few hours as she had some important letters to write.

"Can I go outside and explore mother?" she said.

"Of course, Emily, but don't go too far and don't go near the railway track when there are trains about. I know we will have to cross the track from time to time but trains can be very dangerous".

Clutching her doll Lizzie, Emily took her first steps out of the front door and, with her feet almost invisible in the mist, she carefully walked down the path to a small gate at the front of the property. She could now see that their cottage was set in a small garden with a wooden fence, painted white, running right round it. Turning to look back, the cottage was also freshly painted white and it had an ornately decorated thatched roof. Pink and yellow honeysuckle crept up the cottage walls and on either side of the door stood tall hollyhocks of various colours. There was also a name to one side of the door, 'Honeysuckle Cottage' which Emily thought sounded just right. Walking through the open gate she crossed a small piece of open ground until she came to the single railway track and, remembering what her mother had said, she listened carefully for the sounds of any trains before hurrying over it, taking care not to slip as the wooden sleepers were wet from the mist.

With the sun shining and the birds singing she headed deeper into the cemetery towards all the monuments and gravestones which were now becoming clearer as the mist began to slowly recede in the warmth. As she had seen earlier, the burial plots were everywhere and, as far as the eye could see, there were memorials to the dead. With the sun shining so brightly she didn't feel at all afraid and she wasn't concerned about the prospect of meeting a ghost in broad daylight but she shuddered at the thought of doing this walk at night. She stopped by one of the graves which lay beneath a tall column surmounted by a beautiful angel with outspread wings. She read the inscription and noted that the death was quite recent. The next grave was beneath a large cross, as was the third which was ornately carved to look as if it was ivy covered. Beneath it were fresh flowers indicating that someone had visited it recently. Emily was fascinated by the variety of graves and memorials, some being very simple while others were huge, decorated tombs.

The time slipped past very quickly as she continued her exploration of the cemetery and it was some time before she noticed that the mist had now gone completely. During her wandering she had come to an old shed on the far side of the cemetery where two old men had been sitting, drinking mugs of tea. She smiled as she walked past but they just grunted and eyed her in an odd way. "Do you live here?" she asked.

One of them just grunted but the other one said "No miss, we're having our tea break. We dig the graves here" and he pointed to several picks and shovels leaning against the wall nearby.

"It's lovely and peaceful here" she said.

"That it is. Do you live around here miss?"

Emily explained that they had just moved in to *Honeysuckle Cottage* and she was exploring the cemetery.

"Well don't you get lost" the other gravedigger said in a grumpy tone, "and don't you go wandering around here at night either. There's funny things happen here" and with that word of warning he went back to his tea.

Emily decided he was *Grumpy*. She said goodbye to them and the nice one smiled but Grumpy simply grunted again. She walked on leaving them sitting there in the sun, clearly enjoying their drinks.

Her wandering had eventually brought her to the railway line again which, on its route back to Brookwood station, ran past a high area of ground covered in trees and bushes. Deciding it looked interesting and that she would like to climb to the top for a better view, she once again paused and listened but, hearing no train, she stepped back over the track and began to climb the grassy embankment on the other side. It was quite steep and slippery, and her sheltered life in London hadn't really prepared her for such physical effort but, using her hands and pulling on branches and small bushes, she finally managed to reach the top. She sat down on the grass, brushing some mud from her hands as she looked back across the cemetery. It was strangely beautiful and it seemed almost unreal to think of how different this was compared to waking up in London only yesterday.

From this height she could see that many of the graves were laid out in long straight rows but others were laid out in a circular pattern radiating out from a central point with well-maintained pathways running between them. There were also a lot of trees and bushes including flowering rhododendrons growing along the paths, carefully positioned to provide more seclusion and privacy.

She soon became very conscious of the warm sun and, as she began to feel sleepy from her exertions, she lay back on the grass. She looked up at the sky, thinking about her changed life and relaxed as she watched the birds flying to and fro and a few white clouds drifting by. One bird was hovering overhead and seemed to be singing to her. Emily smiled. She had read books on birds and recognised it as a lark, a bird with a wonderful singing voice. There were also crows meandering across the sky in small groups and, close by, she caught a glimpse of a robin hopping around the bush next to her.

As she drifted into an almost dreamlike trance she suddenly heard a mournful screech coming from high above and Emily was instantly alert. It was no noise she had heard before. Then it came again, a haunting sound that echoed on the gentle breeze. It seemed a long way off but it was a penetrating note which was initially frightening but, at the same time, sounded sad and very lonely or perhaps even lost. The cry came again and Emily stared up into the bright sky trying to see where it was coming from. Then she saw it, high up amongst the clouds. A huge bird, bigger than any bird she had ever seen before, wheeling round in wide circles with giant wings outstretched. There was no motion of its body, no flapping of the wings, just a beautiful bird gracefully gliding on the breeze as it continued to circle round and round, screeching all the time as if it were calling to someone. Emily was spellbound and just stared with her mouth open. If only her mother could see this. As she listened to the bird's cry she noticed that it appeared to be getting lower as it circled. She wasn't sure at first but after it had circled a few more times she was convinced that it was getting lower all the time. She couldn't take her eyes off it as it continued to wheel round, its wings held up in a shallow 'vee' shape, but slowly she realised that it was coming down directly above her and as it got nearer she shrank back under the bush she was sitting next to. The bird book she had read had described birds of prey that ate meat and she was now afraid that the bird had seen her and was coming for her. She could clearly see its feathers now, a brown body, a dark brown band on the underside of the leading edge of the wings and a white band behind this, stretching almost the full spread of the wings. The tail was spread like a fan while the dark wingtips had single feathers protruding from them, almost like fingers. Emily edged further under her bush, ready to jump up and run if it got too close but, just as it seemed she could reach out and touch it, the bird swept past, casting a shadow over her before suddenly pulling in its wings and dropping into the bushes on the hilltop behind her.

Emily was surprised and quite relieved but the bird's sudden disappearance intrigued her. She was still amazed at the size of the bird and very bravely wanted to see it again more closely so she stood up and began to quietly push her way through the bushes in the direction of where the bird had disappeared. The bushes were very thick here and some of them scratched her hands and her clothes but she pressed on until, to her great surprise, she stumbled into a clearing in the middle of a circle of bushes. In the centre of the clearing was what appeared to be a circular brick well about two feet high but what had surprised her was the figure of a young girl sitting on the edge of the well, looking down the shaft.

Emily took a couple of steps forward but then, not wanting to surprise the girl, she called out "Hello."
There was a pause and then the girl slowly turned around to look at her. She seemed slightly surprised and, putting her head on one side, she just said "Hello, how interesting that you saw me here."
Emily looked at her carefully. She had very pale skin, almost white hair and her clothes were also white and shimmered in the sunlight. Her eyes seemed very distant and her expression showed no real emotion, just a kind of sadness.
"I saw you coming" she added, looking at Emily curiously.

Emily wasn't sure how she had seen her but, being very polite, said "I live in *Honeysuckle Cottage* in the cemetery and we have only just moved here. Do you live here?"

The girl thought for a moment before she replied. "Yes, I stay here," but gave no further details.

"I was looking for a big bird" said Emily. "Did you see it land?"

The girl didn't answer directly but said "I know the bird very well. It's quite harmless if that's what you are worried about."

In order to make conversation Emily pulled out the doll from her coat. "This is Lizzie" she said "and my name is Emily"

"Hello Emily. I'm Clara" but she said no more.

Although the girl seemed very nice she didn't seem very communicative so Emily decided it would be down to her to get the conversation going. She told her about their move and her first impressions of the cemetery and the girl seemed to become genuinely interested, asking questions about her family. Emily's face saddened as she told her about her missing father and Clara's eyes softened slightly instead of the earlier cold stare.

"Do you think he will come and join you soon?" she asked.

"We don't know, but we are all very worried and my mother keeps crying."

Clara looked up at the sky as if her thoughts were a long way away and then, putting her head on one side again she said "It's important for families to be together. Don't give up hope Emily. I'm sure he's alive so don't give up hope."

It was a startling thing to say and Emily was taken aback.

Their conversation continued for a long time but Clara remained very enigmatic, not really saying much about herself. She was very interested in Emily and her family, however, and seemed to enjoy hearing about all the interesting things they did together. As they chatted, Emily felt that they had developed a close friendship and she wondered how they might meet again and perhaps play together. Before she could suggest it, however, Clara said that she would have to leave and suggested that Emily return home too in case her mother was worried. It made sense but Emily was disappointed.

"Perhaps we can meet again" she said.

"Oh, I'm sure we will" was the reply.

Chapter 9

North Station

On her way back Emily followed the railway track through the cemetery and when she reached their cottage she could see her mother through the window still writing her letters. Deciding not to disturb her, she continued along the rough pathway towards the station where she could see some activity. As she walked onto the platform a man in uniform came out of an office and, on seeing her, said "Hello, you must be Emily".

She smiled and very politely said "Yes, I'm very pleased to meet you".

He was clearly very impressed with her manner and, just as she was wondering who he was, he introduced himself as George Robinson, the stationmaster.

"You must be Mrs Robinson's husband" she said and he nodded back.

"She's here in the refreshment room if you want to see her" he said and showed her into a small room with a number of tables and comfortable chairs with a serving counter at one end. Mrs Robinson was sweeping the floor.

"A visitor to see you Madge" said Mr Robinson adding "I expect I'll see you later Emily" as he turned and went back out onto the platform.

"Hello Mrs Robinson" said Emily. "I've been all round the cemetery exploring".

Madge smiled and, putting down her broom, said "Well after all that exploring you must be thirsty so come and sit down and I'll fetch you a glass of milk".

Emily sat at a table on one of the comfortable chairs and Madge quickly returned placing a glass of milk in front of her.

"Thank you Mrs Robinson" she said and then, feeling a little embarrassed, she added "I'm afraid I haven't any money with me to pay you".

Madge laughed and said "Goodness me, don't you worry about that my dear. I run this place and if I want to give you a glass of milk that's my business". Then, putting her face close to Emily's she smiled and whispered "and I told you to call me Madge!"

Emily sat quietly, listening as Madge chatted away while preparing some sandwiches. During a pause in the conversation Emily mentioned the girl she had met on the hill which puzzled Madge as she was unaware of any young girls living nearby.

"Perhaps she is one of the mourners come to look at a family grave" she suggested. "I'm surprised she was up there on her own though." Then Emily described the large bird she had seen. Madge stopped what she was doing and looked at her.

"You saw the bird?" she asked, obviously interested. Emily nodded.

"Mmmm" she said "it's been around a lot recently. We've never seen one before and several local people have been quite frightened by it. People think those big birds bring death when they come. Our Tom is an expert on birds and he can tell you more about it."

She went back to work again and continued her conversation.

"It will be nice for you to meet our two boys. In fact our Frank should be fireman on the next train down and it's due soon" she said looking at the clock, "so you should get to meet him". As if on cue, they heard the distant whistle of the approaching train.

"That will be them. Now you will have to run along to the stationmaster's office and watch from there. When the train arrives the mourners will want some privacy".

Madge quickly took off her housecoat revealing a very smart, long black dress with a white lace collar and cuffs. She took a last look around and then, taking Emily's hand, she showed her along the platform to the stationmaster's office.

"There" she said. "You'll be comfortable here and you can watch out the window, but don't be too obvious". She then walked back to the refreshment room as the train appeared from behind some trees around a bend in the track, quietly puffing to itself as it slowly drew into the station.

Emily stood on a chair so she could see out of the window more clearly but kept her head behind a curtain, anxious that her presence would not to intrude on whatever was going to happen next. The train gently came to a standstill and George stepped forward in his formal uniform and opened the door to one of the carriages. He respectfully bowed his head and then helped a group of people out onto the platform, two gentlemen and three ladies. All were dressed in black, the men in suits and frock coats with tall, black hats and the ladies in long black dresses and wearing hats with veils over their faces. Further along the train, two men whom Emily hadn't seen before were removing a coffin from the Hearse Coach and, after placing it on a trolley, they slowly wheeled it into one of the waiting rooms, followed by the five mourners. A priest had also appeared on the platform and he went to join them.

The train crew had stepped down from the engine cab and politely stood on the platform with heads bowed and remained there until the platform was clear whereupon George nodded to the guard. The crew climbed back onto the train while George climbed into the guard's carriage and when the guard waved his flag, the train very quietly pulled forward and puffed out of the station heading for the second station further into the cemetery. As it went past, Emily had a good view of the driver, and a young man she assumed was Frank in the cab while further along the train, she could see more people dressed in black, still seated in another of the carriage compartments. She guessed that the funeral process she had just witnessed would be repeated in a few minutes at the second station.

When the train had gone and it was quiet once again, the coffin was slowly carried out of the station to the private chapel nearby followed by the priest and the funeral party. Emily climbed down off the chair and went back to the refreshment room. Madge was laying out some food on the counter to be ready for when the funeral party returned from the graveside so she asked if there was anything she could do to help.

"Well bless you Emily. If you would like to, could you run a duster over the tables and chairs just in case any soot came in from the engine". Emily picked up a duster and busied herself cleaning the furniture and even polished the doors and door handles, all under her watchful eye. They chatted as they worked, with Madge doing most of the talking.

The door suddenly opened and a voice said "Hello Mum" as two men walked into the room. It was the train crew, Frank and an older man. "We just walked back for a cup of tea before we take the funeral parties back". Madge took out two cups and began making the tea.

"Where's Mr Evans, your guard" she asked.

"Oh he's busy talking to dad so he won't be in."

"This is Emily" Madge said "and she has come to live in the old cottage with her mother and sister". Frank took his hat off and shook Emily's hand which greatly impressed her.

"Hello Emily" he said. He turned and added "This is my driver, Edward. We always work together and he's teaching me everything he knows about engines so I can be a train driver myself one day."

Frank chatted to Emily as they drank their tea while Madge busied herself filling their tin flasks including one for Mr Evans so they would have something to drink on the return journey. Frank told Emily all about his work on the trains and offered to let her step up into the engine cab one day to look at all the controls. Edward asked how long Emily had been staying there but seemed quite disappointed to hear that she had only arrived yesterday. Frank laughed.

"Edward is convinced that on one of the night runs last week he saw a girl dressed in white wandering between the graves as if she were lost or looking for something. It was dark and there was one of those thick mists so I just told him he was imagining things".

Edward just mumbled "I know what I saw, and it was a ghost I'm sure. This cemetery is very creepy at night".

"Oh stop it Edward" said Madge. "You'll frighten Emily and you know there's no such thing as ghosts".

Emily just smiled but couldn't help remembering her own experience of the white figure as she and her mother had walked to the cottage on that first night.

Frank and Edward finished their tea and walked back to their train carrying their flasks. Emily watched them go and decided she should go home too.

"Well, you come back anytime" said Madge and, after saying goodbye, Emily ran home to tell her mother about her exciting day.

Chapter 10

Home Schooling

The next week was an interesting time for Emily as she got used to her new surroundings. She was surprised at how foggy it could get in the cemetery and even when it seemed as if it was going to be a clear day, the fog could easily roll in bringing with it gloom and early darkness.

When she could she spent most days exploring the cemetery or visiting Madge but she soon came to realise how tiring it was becoming owing to the sheer size of the cemetery and all that walking she was doing which made her feel very tired by evening. She often retired to bed early but she still wasn't happy about the nights. She would often be disturbed by the night trains which regularly left her wide awake. She would hear them coming from quite a distance, usually when they left Brookwood and began reversing into the cemetery and past their cottage, and she remained wide awake until the train finally rumbled past again on its return journey back to London. Sometimes she would get up and look out the window to watch the train go by but was surprised how often the fog crept into the cemetery at night, sometimes so thick she couldn't see the train or even the end of the garden. Other times she would just lie there for long periods, listening to the silence and then the voices would come. It was just low murmuring in the background but she couldn't make out any words. Of course it could have been just her imagination or the wind blowing through the trees. The trains and voices had upset her initially but she didn't want to mention it to her mother as she knew that her mother already had enough problems to worry about.

Mrs Williams was still terribly worried about her husband and had many dark days when she would just sit quietly for long periods, feeling depressed or even crying, and withdrawing into a little world of her own. She was also worried about their lack of money and was very unsure of what the future might hold for them. She wrote several letters to the private detective that her husband had hired in London hoping that his investigations had been successful but the replies were always discouraging and no comfort to her. On one of her better days, however, she decided that, if only for Emily's sake, she needed to do something more positive to occupy herself. It wasn't long before she had an idea. Madge had quickly become a regular visitor to *Honeysuckle Cottage*, cleaning the rooms, food shopping and preparing meals that could be left in the kitchen to warm up when required. With Madge's help Mrs Williams had quickly turned the dusty room at the back of the cottage into a school room and within a few days Emily was settled into her routine of classes in the morning and playtime in the afternoon. Mrs Williams enjoyed being occupied and quickly realised that she got a lot of pleasure out of teaching her in a variety of interesting subjects. One of Emily's favourite lessons was art which was not surprising as her mother was a very good artist who enjoyed watercolour painting. In fact it had been one of her favourite pastimes but over the past few years she had neglected it. Now, however, using it as the basis for art lessons, both she and Emily could enjoy painting once again.

"You know Emily, the scenery around the cemetery is quite beautiful so I might use the location as a subject for some paintings."

In no time at all she created some unusual yet stunning landscape paintings of the cemetery, some at sunset, some at sunrise with a mist rolling over the tombs, and others on bright, uplifting, sunny days.

Mrs Williams had a natural talent for painting and in no time at all she had a number of finished pictures. They were quite eye catching so it wasn't surprising that one day, as Madge was chatting while washing up in the kitchen, she spotted some these paintings drying on the table. She stopped and looked at them carefully.

"Did you paint these" she said.

Mrs Williams nodded. "It's my hobby" she said. "It's very relaxing and it helps to take my mind off other things".

Madge was very impressed and continued to look at them.

She hesitated for a moment and then asked "If you have time, would you paint one for me to put up in the refreshment room?"

Mrs Williams was surprised and laughed saying "Of course I would Madge, but I really don't think they are that good. If you want, why don't you take those ones on the table."

Madge was very pleased and Mrs Williams thought nothing more of it.

The following day, Madge spent some time carefully putting the paintings on the walls of the refreshment rooms at both of the stations. "There" she said to herself. "That brightens up the place. Our customers never say very much so it will give them something to look at while they sit here."

For the next few days the weather was miserable with heavy rain and strong winds so Emily was not able to go exploring again which was very disappointing. She contented herself with playing in the parlour or sitting on the window seat reading some old books she had found lying on a shelf. Madge had asked her what she was reading and Emily, read out the title.

"It's called *Vanity Fair*" she said "and I found another called *Jane Eyre* but to be honest neither of them is very interesting."

"Let me look" said Madge and she picked up the books and flicked through them. "Mmm, I'm not surprised you are not interested Emily, this type of book is not really for you. I will bring you some of Tom's old adventure stories tomorrow and I'm sure you will find them far more suitable."

With that, Madge put the two books up on a high shelf, out of reach.

True to her word, she turned up the following day with several books hidden under her coat to keep them dry as it was still raining. Emily was excited as she looked through the titles, some of them having pictures of explorers on the front covers but Madge quickly said "You must put them away for now because you have to do your lessons first." Later that day Emily chose one of the books titled *Coral Island* and immediately became engrossed in the story.

Chapter 11

A Forgery Uncovered

The weather continued to be terrible for several more days and they were surprised when one afternoon, in the middle of a torrential downpour, there was a knock on the door.

"Who on earth is that" said Mother as she opened the door and there on the doorstep was a very bedraggled postman looking extremely wet and unhappy.

"Parcel for you Mrs Williams" he said and handed over a rather damp package.

"Oh Mr Jones" she said "You're soaked through. Come in and sit by the fire until this rain passes over."

Mr Jones looked up at the black clouds and said "Well I'm not supposed to Mrs Williams but I don't mind if I do" and he stepped inside. He removed his hat and waterproof and left them hanging by the door and then walked over to the fire where he stood rather self-consciously but clearly enjoying the warmth.

"Sit down Mr Jones and I'll make us all some tea."

Emily carried on reading while they chatted as her *Coral Island* book was getting really exciting. "How wonderful" she thought "to have an adventure, but it never happens to people like me."

The rain clouds eventually passed over and after thanking Mrs Williams for her hospitality, the postman went on his way. Mother sat down by the fire and, opening the parcel, she saw a letter from the bank manager and a box of official-looking papers. The letter said that the papers may be of interest to Mrs Williams, particularly the recent, unexpected withdrawals from the account. The papers were obviously very important and kept Mother busy all afternoon, reading the documents and making notes. Emily stayed out of her way and just played with her doll and read more of her book so as not to disturb her. They had a late tea and Emily finally decided to go to bed early as Mrs Williams was clearly going to be working into the night, writing more letters.

Emily didn't sleep well again that night. She had heard the Necropolis train come through the cemetery on the usual night run around 10 o' clock and it had left again a short time later. She was lying there, half asleep, trying to remember her dream. She had been in a long dark tunnel and in the background the voices had come to her again, just like before but louder. There was a heavy feeling in the air and, as she struggled to recall more of the dream, a bright flash suddenly lit up the room followed a few seconds later by a loud clap of thunder. She was instantly fully awake. There was a storm coming and Emily didn't like storms. She got out of bed and walked over to the window to close the curtains but couldn't resist glancing out. The rain was beating down heavily again and the cemetery was dark, the moon hidden behind the heavy clouds so she could see nothing on the ground but then came another flash which momentarily lit up the scene like daylight. In just one second she clearly saw the wet graves and tombstones throwing frightening shadows across the ground but she recoiled when she saw several white figures, standing by the graves and staring up at her. She rushed back to her bed just as the thunder came, louder than before, and quickly pulled the covers over her head. As she lay there shaking she heard the bedroom door quietly open and gripped the covers more tightly. She held her breath as the sound of footsteps quietly crossed the floor to the foot of the bed and paused. A quiet voice then said "It's alright Emily. I will stay here with you" and her mother sat on the bed, gently pulling the covers down, off her head.

The following morning the rain had finally stopped and the storm had passed over, leaving a fresh scent of honeysuckle and wet grass in the air. It was Saturday and there were no lessons so Emily decided she would go exploring again if her mother didn't need her for anything. It was a day when Madge wasn't coming in so she helped her mother prepare breakfast. A letter had arrived by the early post and as they ate their toast, Mrs Williams opened it and read it with great interest. It was from the detective in London

Dear Mrs Williams
Further to your recent enquiries regarding our investigation into Mr Jack Griffiths I am pleased to inform you that we finally have some news for you.

We have discovered that he has frequently changed his name over the years in order to cover his tracks which has made our investigations that much more difficult.

We can now inform you, however, that he has indeed acquired a long criminal record for theft, fraud and forgery and has been to prison several times. The Metropolitan Police still have an outstanding warrant for his arrest relating to further crimes he has committed.

I will gather the relevant information and send it to you but I thought you might like to know in advance that the man is not to be trusted.

I remain your servant

D N Davies

City Detective Agency

It was the news she had hoped for. An indication that Mr Williams' partner was not a man to be trusted. She was very excited and decided to re-examine the papers from the bank again in light of this new information. As they finished breakfast and were clearing everything away, Emily asked if she could go out and explore as she hadn't been out for so long. Mrs Williams said she was happy for her to go as long as she was careful as everything would be wet and muddy but added that she might like to call in to see Madge on the way to ask if she needed any help. Emily thought this was a lovely idea as she so much enjoyed chatting to her and doing the important work of polishing the tables.

Mrs Williams then sat down with her box of papers and, spreading them out, she looked at them more carefully. Yes, there was something not quite right. She was very familiar with her husband's signature but the signature at the bottom of several of the letters was very slightly different. It was cleverly done and good enough to pass a casual glance but as she studied them more closely she became convinced that the letters were not his.

Chapter 12

A Trip to the Well

The sun was shining brightly as Emily skipped along the path to the station carefully avoiding the puddles and the air was filled with the sounds of so many birds singing in the trees, almost as if they too were pleased the storm had passed. She wondered if she might see the big bird again today and then her thoughts went back to the friend she had found on the hill. An unusual girl but she seemed very nice.

Approaching the station Emily was still thinking about her week and felt very pleased with herself, so much so that she began a conversation with her doll.

"How odd Lizzie that I have got used to living here so quickly, and I am even getting used to the trains passing day and night and lots of bodies being buried all around us."

She was right, of course. For a rather shy and sometimes nervous child, living there was a challenge. It certainly was a strange, if not unique experience and Emily had done well to adjust to the changes in her life. In truth, she didn't want to admit to anyone, including Lizzie, that she was still having restless nights. Her experience of last night when the night special passed through hadn't really bothered her at all and even the storm had been bearable with her mother sitting on the bed stroking her hair but she gave an involuntary shudder as she recalled those mysterious figures in the cemetery. As she walked along the path she held Lizzie in front of her and continued her conversation adding "Kate once told me that you can get used to anything eventually so I suppose it must be true."

When Emily finally arrived at the station she could see that the door to the refreshment room was open. As she walked in she was surprised to see that Madge had a young boy with her, about her age. He was helping to move some tables and stopped when he saw her walk in. "Hello Emily" called Madge. "This is my youngest boy Tom. There, you have met the whole family now".

She and Tom said hello to each other but it was obvious that they were both being a bit shy. Emily then spoke up. "I've come to see if you want any help Madge".

"Why thank you dear" was the reply. "Do you want to polish again."

Emily was happy with this and after picking up a duster from the counter she carefully went round all the furniture while Tom continued to move the tables and some chairs.

Summoning up his courage Tom suddenly said "My mum says you like birds" and then quickly looked down again, embarrassed, as he busied himself with a difficult chair.

"Yes" said Emily, glad of something to break the silence. "I saw a really big one the other day but I didn't know what it was".

Tom was instantly interested and they both stopped working as she described the bird to him.

"Mmm" he said. "That sounds like a buzzard. I've seen one before but not round here. That's very unusual."

He asked where she had seen it and Emily tried to describe the hill where she had been sitting.

Madge smiled to herself as they chatted and said "The jobs are just about finished now so why don't you two run off and look for that bird". They thought that was an excellent idea and in no time at all they were out the door, over the railway track and hurrying in the direction of the hill.

It took a while to get there as several times Tom stopped to point out something of interest which Emily would easily have missed. He showed her several bird nests in the surrounding bushes and trees, some containing eggs while one of them contained three young blackbirds which they were careful not to disturb. He was clearly very knowledgeable and keen on all forms of wildlife, not just birds. He seemed to know so much and Emily was feeling a little embarrassed at how little she was able to contribute to the conversation. He then showed her a caterpillar nest on a low branch, a slow worm half hidden under a stone, and he even spotted a large toad sitting on a damp piece of grass behind one of the graves. Emily wasn't keen to touch it but Tom gently touched its back and it slowly walked away into the longer grass where it sat down in a puddle.

"Aren't they supposed to hop?" asked Emily.

"No" said Tom. "That's what frogs do. Toads walk".

They eventually reached the railway track and, crossing over, they began to clamber up the hill. Tom was very agile and quickly left Emily behind as she kept slipping back on the muddy grass but, when he saw her struggling, he came back and helped pull her up. At the top they stopped to get their breath and look back over the cemetery.

"I haven't been up here before" he admitted. "In fact I haven't spent any time at this end of the cemetery so this is really exciting".

This pleased Emily a great deal as this was finally something she knew about and she would be able to show him.

"Come on" she said "it's this way to the well" and with that she began to push her way through the bushes. They seemed thicker than before and she had to push very hard to get through them. In fact the bushes were so thick that she soon began to worry that she had lost her way but she pressed on in the hope of recognising something that she remembered. Tom was close behind her but she heard him stumble and call out

"Hang on, I've lost my shoe" and he sat down to put it on again.

Emily didn't stop though as she was now becoming convinced that she had taken the correct route and almost immediately she was able to breathe a sigh of relief as the bushes opened out into the now familiar clearing.

There, in the centre was the well and sitting on the stone wall was Clara. Emily was surprised and exclaimed "Oh" at which Clara turned round. Her face was white and her stare was vacant as if she were looking into the distance but she obviously recognised Emily and, putting her head to one side, said quietly "Hello, have you come to see me again?" Emily smiled. She was pleased that Clara was there and very much wanted to talk to her again as she had enjoyed their previous conversation together.
"Yes" she said "and I've brought a friend with me".
For the briefest moment Clara's eyes flashed and she looked disappointed but just then there was a thud behind Emily and she turned round to see Tom fall out of the bushes, still struggling to tie his shoelace.
"Thank goodness" he said. "I can see what I'm doing now." He looked up and said "Who were you talking to?"
Emily turned back towards the well but Clara had gone. She stared, unbelieving at first but then, in a moment of panic, she ran forward thinking Clara must have fallen into the well. She reached the little wall and looked over the edge but was surprised to see, just a little way down the shaft, a sturdy metal grille.

She was still looking at it when Tom arrived saying "Gosh, this is very interesting". He joined her looking over the edge. "What are we looking for?"

"My friend Clara was here but she disappeared and I thought she might have been frightened by your noisy arrival and fallen in."

Tom was slightly offended by the suggestion but he simply replied "Well she didn't fall through that rusty old grille did she".

Emily looked around hoping to see Clara hiding in the bushes but Tom was busily investigating the low circular wall. Eventually she came back to him and he surprised her by saying "You know, I don't think this is a well at all". Emily looked surprised but listened as Tom explained. "There's no bucket or even a place where a bucket winder might have been attached."

He picked up a stone and said "listen to this" and then dropped the stone through the grille. After a few seconds a loud thud reverberated up the shaft. "See" he said. "No splash so there's no water at the bottom".

He then noticed that the circular grille was hinged on one side. Like the grille, the hinges were very rusty but when Tom gripped it with his fingers and pulled it upwards, it lifted slightly.

"Give me a hand" he said and with them both pulling together, the grille slowly lifted up, the hinges creaking all the way, until it eventually stood upright exposing the full darkness of the shaft.

As Tom leaned over to peer down the shaft there was a sudden, piercing scream and the sun was blotted out by a dark shadow as a huge bird swept over them, so low that they both had to duck. Emily cried out but Tom just watched, amazed, as the bird turned and dived down at them again before lifting up over the trees and, with a few slow flaps of its wings, disappeared from view.

"That was the bird I was telling you about" said Emily. Tom was still staring into the distance with his mouth open, transfixed by the close up spectacle he had just witnessed.

"That was incredible" he eventually said. "It was a buzzard but I have never seen one that close. They usually keep their distance from people so it was very odd behaviour, almost as if it was attacking us."

Emily's heart was still pounding but Tom quickly recovered and looking back down the shaft he said "Look, there's a metal ladder set into the wall". Emily felt it and, although it looked rusty, it seemed quite secure.

"We can climb down it" Tom said excitedly but Emily wasn't so sure. Before she could stop him Tom climbed over the wall and, grasping the ladder in both hands, he started to climb down, checking his weight on each rung as he went.

"I'll wait here" said Emily "but don't go far Tom as it might be dangerous".

In no time at all Tom was lost in the darkness. Emily stood there, looking into the black hole and getting more worried by the minute. There might be something horrible living down there in the dark, about to grab Tom. It might even climb up the ladder to get her. She was just about to call out for Tom to come back when she heard scraping on the rungs as if something was climbing up the shaft. She stepped back but suddenly Tom's head reappeared at the top of the ladder. He hopped back over the wall and said "Well that was no good. It's so dark you can't see a thing so we will have to come back with a lantern to explore it properly". Tom was clearly very excited at the prospect but Emily wasn't so happy about climbing down that hole so she just stayed silent.

Chapter 13

An Interesting Discovery

After they carefully replaced the grille over the well, Emily and Tom walked back through the bushes and down the hill to the railway track. A church clock was striking 11 o' clock in the distance so Tom had a bright idea and said "Let's walk along the track to the mainline station. I haven't explored this part of the track before and there should be a cemetery train arriving soon so we can watch the engine change ends on the run around loop". They set off along the track towards Brookwood station, hurrying to get there before the train arrived, and as they walked Tom told Emily all he knew about buzzards.

"You heard what my mum thinks" he said. "My mum reckons that buzzards are harbingers of death".

Emily didn't like the thought of that and was still thinking about it when Tom stopped. "That's odd" he said "look at that". He pointed ahead to a large lever at the side of the track. "That's a points lever. What's that doing in the middle of the cemetery?"

"What's a points lever" asked Emily.

As they walked forward to investigate Tom explained that when the lever was pulled it moved parts of the railway track from side to side to switch trains from one line to another.

"They obviously have points at each end of the passing loop to route the train onto one track or the other but just here there is only one track" he said "so there is no need for any points".

When they arrived at the lever, they could see that it was very rusty and most of the red paint on the handle had flaked off. What interested Tom, however, was the now apparent explanation for the lever as another railway track could be seen running off to one side. It looked very old and was covered in soil and small bushes, almost hiding it from view but although outwardly it looked neglected, the top surface of the metal rails was still shiny. Tom looked more closely at the points lever and again, despite looking as if it hadn't been used for years, the mechanism was well oiled and when he lifted the lever it moved easily.

"I think I know what this is" he said as the realisation dawned. "My dad told me that some years ago the railway company started a railway line extension from here to Guildford but they abandoned it and the line was eventually built from Woking to Guildford instead".

"Why did they abandon it?" asked Emily. Tom thought for a moment, trying to remember the conversation he had with his father.

"My dad said it became too dangerous because they had to dig a tunnel at some point and they had a lot of accidents with parts of the roof collapsing".

He suddenly stopped and a large grin crossed his face. Then to Emily's surprise he started jumping up and down shouting "I've got it, I've got it!"

"What is it Tom" she said. "Oh please tell me".

Tom looked at her triumphantly and said in a rush "That well you found on the hill, it wasn't a well at all. It was a ventilation shaft leading down to the old tunnel".

Just at that moment they heard the whistle of the approaching Necropolis train so they quickly stepped off the track and watched as the engine appeared, slowly pulling the carriages round the bend from Brookwood station. It was puffing and hissing quietly and as it drew near they could see driver Sykes looking out of the cab at them. Emily was about to wave when he turned back and said something bringing his fireman, O'Hare, to the cab door and they both glared at the two children as the train drew near.

As the carriages rolled past, Emily and Tom just stood quietly. They could see the parties of mourners inside, all dressed in black and then the special Hearse Carriages which held the coffins. It would be a sad day for them thought Emily. The two children watched as the last carriage disappeared round the bend heading towards North Station and the silence returned once again.

"That train crew doesn't seem very nice" said Emily.

"No" replied Tom. "Sykes wasn't quite so bad until that fireman O'Hare came to work with him last year and since then they have been a miserable pair. They always prefer to do the night runs because they get more pay but since they started doing it my dad says there have been some very strange goings on in the cemetery."

Emily waited for him to explain but he just stood there quietly thinking.

Eventually Emily broke the silence. "Where does this track lead then."

Tom wasn't sure but said "Let's follow it and find out". They had to walk beside the track as the wooden sleepers between the rails were covered in rocks and mud in places with small bushes growing amongst them but Tom noticed that the surface of the rails still remained shiny as if they had been recently used. They followed the track through a small forest area with trees growing on each side, almost encroaching on the rails and soon the thick tree canopy overhead covered the tracks completely making it very dark. As they pressed on, in front of them the steep face of the hillside suddenly appeared out of the gloom. The railway track continued into a dark tunnel entrance but it was blocked off by a heavy wooden gate that was padlocked. On the gate were two old signs saying *DANGER* and *KEEP OUT*.

"Well that proves it" said Tom walking up to the gate and looking through the bars. "This is the disused tunnel entrance".

Emily thought for a moment and said "Well it's lucky you didn't climb too far down that ventilation shaft. The roof could have collapsed on you."

Tom shrugged, still peering into the darkness and said "I'd love to look inside but we can't get through this gate. Come on, we might as well go back now and find mum. The mourners should have gone to the church by now so she might make us a drink."

As he turned round something caught his attention. He noticed that the padlock on the gate was a new one and once again, it had been freshly oiled.

"Mmm" he thought. "That's odd. Dad told me the tunnel was closed years ago so no-one should have been using this gate recently".

When they got back to North Station there was no-one around except Madge busily making a fresh pot of tea. She was glad they were back because she had some news.

"Your sister, Kate has arrived and your mum would like you back home straight away".

Emily's face lit up. She had missed Kate and was so pleased that she was now here. She rushed off home leaving Tom looking after her and feeling very disappointed.

Chapter 14

Kate Arrives

When Emily arrived home there was a horse drawn carriage waiting at the gate which would normally have attracted her attention but, ignoring it, she rushed past and as she ran up the garden path, Kate stepped out of the front door, swept her up in her arms and swung her round several times, laughing and hugging her.

"I've missed you" they both said together and they laughed again.

"I've so much to tell you" Emily said as they went back into the house.

Kate had arrived earlier that morning and, in addition to the driver, she had been escorted by Maria, the maid with whom she had travelled to the south coast. One of Kate's cousins from Lyme Regis where she had been staying had also accompanied them. She had been very happy staying in their big house and had spent many relaxing hours with all of her cousins wandering along the cliff paths or on the beach but she couldn't put thoughts of her father out of her mind. Eventually she decided she should really be with her own family and so arrangements had been made to bring her to Brookwood. As Kate led Emily into the sitting room, she introduced her to cousin Rebecca who was about the same age as Kate but taller with long dark hair gathered under her hat. She was also introduced to the driver of the carriage who had been invited in for a cup of tea and was looking slightly uncomfortable as he sat with Maria in a corner, not being used to invitations to join *the gentry*.

Mrs Williams explained that as the London house had now been closed up, only two of the servants had been retained temporarily to look after it and Maria had been re-employed, working for Rebecca's family in Lyme Regis. The reunion with Kate had been a wonderful time and, after Rebecca and Maria had left in the carriage, Emily showed her upstairs to their shared room and helped her to unpack her clothes. She was desperate to tell her all about their new home and couldn't stop talking about the people she had met and of her adventures in the cemetery.

"My goodness" said Kate when she finally managed to get a word in. "You have had an exciting time. You must take me out tomorrow and show me around".

The next few days were a buzz of activity as Kate settled in to the new routine and Emily showed her around the house and the cemetery although they didn't go as far as the tunnel. Kate had already met Madge at the cottage but Emily was anxious for her to visit North Station to see her at work there and to show how she helped around the refreshment room by dusting and polishing. During their visit to the station Madge said that Emily had been very helpful to her as there was always so much work to be done whereupon Kate laughed and said "Well I'm sure I could lend a hand too if you need me".

Madge stopped what she was doing and looked at her. "Are you serious?" she asked.

"Why of course" said Kate. "I don't think I will have much to do around here otherwise, what with Emily off exploring all the time and mother looking after her legal matters and spending her time painting".

Madge came over and sat down at the table where Kate had been sitting. She looked Kate in the eye and said "You are a very attractive young lady, very polite and presentable, and from what I have seen you are very intelligent too." Kate could feel herself blushing but Madge went on. "As you know, we have two stations here and each one has a refreshment room. It's very difficult for me trying to be in two places at once, rushing from one to the other to keep the funeral parties happy so I need someone to look after South Station for me and be the manager there. Would you do it?"

Kate was quite taken aback and Emily's eyes went wide. "You could be a manager" she said.

"I don't know" stammered Kate. "Do you think I would be able to do it Madge?"

"Well of course you could, a clever girl like you, and the company would pay you too. It wouldn't be much but every little helps" and with that she sat back while Kate thought about it very carefully. In the end, although she was still apprehensive, Kate thought it would be an interesting challenge and the money would help the family too, so she said yes, as long as her mother approved. Madge clapped her hands with pleasure and said "Let's go and speak to her now, and if she says yes I will sort out a black uniform for you. You could start tomorrow!"

And so began a new period in the lives of the Williams family at Brookwood. Mrs Williams thought it was an excellent idea for Kate to manage the other station and Madge quickly found her a long black dress with lace trimming just like her own and which only needed a few small adjustments to fit. She and Madge spent several days working together but Kate quickly became familiar with the routines and confident when dealing with the customers. Madge then decided that she didn't need any more instruction and left her to manage the South Station on her own, visited regularly by George who kept a fatherly eye on her.

Kate's working time was usually during the morning and only sometimes during the early afternoon so it largely coincided with Emily's school time. Emily still enjoyed her lessons with her mother. It was always very relaxed and Mother was a very knowledgeable person. She was also a very good teacher, making the lessons fun whenever she could. Painting was still Emily's favourite lesson and she would often sit in the front garden with her mother painting the cemetery scenery. What she really looked forward to, however, were the afternoons when she would go out and meet Tom to play and explore or just spend time together. They had not gone back to the tunnel as Tom's father, George, had forbidden it when Tom told him of their discovery.

"That tunnel is very dangerous" he said "so you stay away from it young man."

Tom was disappointed but accepted the advice. He and Emily were now spending a lot of time together and he would frequently visit her house and would sometimes have tea with the family. Mrs Williams thought he was such a nice boy and was pleased that Emily had found such a good friend.

When there were no funeral parties around Emily would often go to the station to chat to Kate and help with polishing which she still did for Madge as well. The three of them got on so well together and as the trains only came twice a day on average, there was always lots of relatively free time for tidying the kitchen, stock checks and general administration, particularly in the afternoons. When the mourners had all gone back on the last train, Madge would often wander over to the South

Station with Emily and the three of them would sit and have a cup of tea to talk about their day.

Kate also had another regular visitor. When Madge's son, Frank, had first arrived at South Station and seen Kate, he had become instantly besotted with her. He thought she was the most beautiful girl he had ever seen and looked forward to his train journeys to Brookwood where he took every opportunity to hang around the refreshment room talking to her. Madge was quite amused by it and one day, when she had no mourners at her station, Madge had walked over to South Station to see them. She found Edward the driver and Mr Evans sitting on a chair drinking large cups of tea but Frank was leaning on the counter watching Kate as she prepared some sandwiches.

Madge pretended to be indignant and said in a loud voice "Haven't you got an engine to look after?"

Frank was completely taken by surprise and, quickly stepping back, he fell over a chair in his haste while Kate kept her head down and chuckled under her breath.

"Don't you need to fill the boiler or polish the brass handles or something?"

Frank recovered himself and just said "Yes mum" and rushed out the door with Madge calling after him "And why don't you come and see me anymore."

Driver Edward laughed as he watched Frank leave. "He's very much taken with the lass here" he said.

"I know" said Madge "but he needs to keep his mind on his work". She then whispered to Kate "He does like you, you know" and Kate smiled and blushed. She just said "He's very nice".

Chapter 15

Picnic in the Fog

Emily and Tom had noticed the developing friendship between Kate and Frank too. As they were walking through the trees at the back of the cemetery one day Tom said "Do you know, I saw them holding hands yesterday".

Emily thought to herself for a moment and said "Why would they do that?"

"I don't know" said Tom "but it all looks daft to me".

As they stepped out of the trees, Emily could see *Honeysuckle Cottage* beyond the railway line, sitting in its little garden. Emily had grown to love living here and as she looked at it, she realised how pretty and cosy it was and how it now gave her such a warm feeling of security. As she looked, she saw the post boy arrive on his bicycle. "Unusual" she thought. "It's not the usual postman so it must be a telegram."

Tom had suggested that they climb up the hill again as he was desperate to get another close up view of the buzzard. They had seen it on several occasions when they were in that part of the cemetery but it was always flying high, almost as if it were avoiding them.

They had taken a small picnic with them that Madge had prepared and when they arrived at the ventilation shaft, they sat down in the clearing and opened the bag. There were beef sandwiches, some bread and jam, apples, pears, and two bottles of lemonade.

"That looks lovely" said Emily and they both tucked in. As they sat there Emily kept looking around hoping she would see Clara while Tom kept looking at the sky hoping to see the buzzard. Both were disappointed, however, and just contented themselves eating their food. As they talked, Tom mentioned that his school holidays were starting the following week.

"That means there will be no school for four weeks" he said with a big grin. He was clearly looking forward to all that free time but Emily was left wondering if she would get a school holiday too. As they were eating they both commented on how dark it was getting. In fact, some odd wisps of fog were drifting past the ventilation shaft in the centre of the clearing. When they finished their meal Tom walked over to the shaft and looked over the wall.

"That's strange" he said. "There's a smell of smoke in the shaft."

Emily came over and sniffed. "Yes" she said, "it's like the smell of a steam train."

They thought about that until Emily said "Well the train did a night run last night. I heard it go past so perhaps some smoke blew into the tunnel and the smell is still hanging around."

As they set off for home it was late afternoon and, rather unusually, the growing darkness was becoming very noticeable now and there was a definite chill in the air. While climbing down the hill they found themselves walking into a rapidly forming mist, initially beginning in the distance but now fast becoming a thick fog surrounding them and making Emily feel very uncomfortable. She was beginning to lose her sense of direction and Tom was beginning to look concerned too.

"The fog comes in very quickly round here doesn't it" he said at last.

"Yes, it's not very nice is it" she replied, more to break the eerie silence than anything else.

As they walked on through the thickening fog Emily suddenly thought she heard a noise behind them and turned but could see nothing further than just a few yards. There were few sounds now and the few noises they did hear were deadened by the fog but she was sure she had heard a twig break on the path. Perhaps it was her imagination? They walked on in silence now but then they both stopped again when an odd scraping noise could be heard behind them followed by footsteps which seemed to be following them. Emily wanted to run but Tom grabbed her hand and bravely stood his ground. The footsteps were getting nearer and Tom called out "Who's there?" There was no reply but the scraping got louder and a dark shape began to appear through the fog. It was indistinct but getting nearer all the time so Emily closed her eyes and gripped Tom's hands tighter. A figure suddenly loomed out of the fog and stopped in front of them.

"Didn't expect this" a voice said.

Tom recognised him immediately. It was one of the gravediggers and he was carrying a spade.

"Hello Jim" he said with relief in his voice. "We wondered who it was following us".

"Well don't hang around here. You best get yourselves home quickly as this is going to get very thick tonight."

He nodded to Emily and walked on, half dragging the spade behind him, and quickly disappeared into the fog.

Chapter 16

The Vault

Over breakfast the following morning Emily was still disappointed about not seeing Clara. She had woken again during the night and gone to her bedroom window to see how thick the fog was and found she couldn't even see the front gate. She had jumped when a large white shape drifted across the garden and had rushed back to bed but as she lay there she convinced herself that it was probably a barn owl. She didn't go back to sleep straight away and as she lay there she suddenly had a thought.

Whenever she had gone to the hill with Tom, Clara didn't appear. Yes, she thought, that was interesting. The only time she had ever seen Clara was when she was there on her own. Perhaps, she thought, she should try an experiment by going to the hill on her own next time and not mention it to Tom.

As they sat eating the lovely breakfast Madge had prepared for them – eggs, bacon, fresh bread and a large pot of tea - Mrs Williams told Emily and Kate that she had received a telegram from Uncle John. He had arrived in South Africa a few days earlier and had immediately gone to the mine to find out what was happening. She did not tell them everything that was contained in the telegram, however, as it had really upset her when she first read it and, not wanting the girls to know, she had retired to her bedroom for a while to be alone.

Apparently Mr Williams' partner, Griffiths, had not been pleased by Uncle John's arrival and had been reluctant to show him the tunnel collapse at the mine because of what he called *safety concerns*. Uncle John would have none of it, however, and had insisted on visiting the mine where he quickly came to realise how little had been done to try and rescue anyone who might have been trapped. Ten miners were missing behind the rock fall including Mr Williams. Griffiths had emphasised that digging had started straight away but said it was slow, dangerous work. He also added, rather callously, that after all this time anyone buried in the mine was probably dead anyway, and any further rescue work would prevent the workers from doing their normal job of digging out the diamond ore. Uncle John, however, was convinced there was still hope, stressing that the miners always took food with them and there would be plenty of air and natural water deep in the mine. As a major investor in the mine he insisted that more people were put on the rescue task immediately, a suggestion that Griffiths opposed but the other mine workers agreed and, having many friends still missing, they rebelled and, ignoring Griffiths' objections, they all went back to the rescue work leaving Griffiths angry and frustrated, but quite unable to stop them.

Although she was only given a shortened version, Emily listened to her mother in silence, clutching her doll Lizzie to her chest. Mrs Williams read the telegram once more to herself and then, looking at her, said "We mustn't give up hope. I'm sure Uncle John will do everything he can to find your father." Emily jumped down off her chair and gave her mother a big hug.

The news in the telegram was quite distressing and they sat at the table in silence for a while. Eventually Madge brought a fresh pot of tea through and Mrs Williams asked her to join them. As she was now such a good friend, almost like an elderly aunt, she was often asked to join the family at the table so they could catch up on each other's news. Madge was particularly interested to overhear the news in the telegram and, perhaps for the first time, she began to appreciate the full depth of pain and worry the family had been going through.

The fog was still thick outside so Emily went through to the parlour and sat on her window seat where she spent the morning reading her book. She kept looking out in the hope it would clear but it was still thick at lunchtime. She desperately wanted to go out so after their meal she put on her coat and told her mother she was going for a walk. Mrs Williams looked at the fog and was concerned but eventually relented and said Emily mustn't go far and was to come back soon.

As Emily walked out into the cemetery she was shocked at how little visibility there was because of the fog and, after tripping over an old gravestone that she had failed to see, she decided that this was definitely not a good day to go to the hill. Instead she thought she might just get some exercise by walking to the centre of the cemetery where she remembered a large memorial statue stood in a circular ring of graves. Once again she noticed how the fog muffled all the normal sounds around her making it eerily quiet. She soon became lost in the many pathways and avenues but wasn't at all concerned and, remembering what her mother had said in one of her art lessons, she took time to carefully study the graves and tombs as she went, observing the fine detail of the ornately carved stones.

She eventually came to a very large tomb but, just as she was passing it, she heard a noise. She stopped to listen and heard it again, like a banging coming from inside. There was a heavy wooden door on the front of the tomb and as the banging continued she was sure the door had just moved. Emily could feel the hair on the back of her neck begin to rise. Yes, it was moving and she became frozen to the spot when the hinges started to creak and a hand appeared around the door, slowly pushing it open. A figure suddenly appeared in the doorway.
"Hello again miss."

Emily had fully expected some supernatural apparition to appear and was greatly relieved to find it was only Jim the gravedigger standing there with an oil can in his hand.

"Hello Jim" she said. "What are you doing in there?"

"There's to be another burial later this week in this family vault" he explained "so I'm just making sure the door opens properly and that it's tidy inside. It's a lot easier than digging a hole" he added with a chuckle.

Emily peered into the dark doorway but couldn't see anything.

"You can go in and have a look if you want" Jim said "but don't touch anything. I've run out of oil so I'm off to my shed to get some more."

With that he walked off into the fog and Emily was left on her own.

She was curious and really wanted to look inside the vault but she knew that people were interred in places like this and she was afraid of what the bodies might look like. She thought about it for a long time, fascinated by the inviting doorway but couldn't bring herself to go over to it while on her own.

"If only Tom were here" she thought.

She would have to go home soon so she made a determined decision to just have a quick look before heading back. She took a few steps forward until she was standing in the doorway and slowly leaned forward. It felt cold and damp and was very dark inside but as her eyes gradually got used to it she could see five coffins stacked around the walls, some in quite good condition but two of them old and damaged. One, which looked as if it had been there for many years, even had a side panel rotted away and she could see white bones protruding through the hole.

Emily was now quite scared but her curiosity drove her on and she couldn't resist stepping inside the vault. As she turned to look back at the wall by the door behind her she saw a stone shelf and lying on it was a skeleton, it's mouth wide open. She stepped back in horror, which took her further into the vault and then, quietly at first, the voices started. This time it wasn't just mumbling, she could hear what sounded like laughter, and the laughing sounded very unpleasant. One of the voices was quietly whispering "This one's special" while another voice whispered "She can see us" followed by more laughter.

The fog was drifting into the vault now like a river flowing through the doorway and forming a thick blanket across the floor with swirls of fog rising up to create strange shapes. Common sense said she should go but she couldn't move as she watched, fascinated by the dancing shapes. Suddenly, another voice came into her head, rising above the laughter and with a sense of great urgency.

"Get out Emily. Get out now!"

Emily snapped out of her trance-like state and didn't wait. She began to run towards the door just as it began to creak and started closing. At the same time, one of the skeleton's arms which had been lying across its rib cage suddenly slipped down to stretch across the floor as if blocking her path while the skull rolled to one side, as if staring at her.

Emily gave a stifled scream but continued to rush headlong towards the rapidly closing door, throwing herself through the narrowing gap just in time as it slammed shut. There was no further hesitation. She ran, without looking back, rushing through the fog as fast as she could, terrified of what might be following her. She ran and ran with no sense of direction, turning left and right as she went, but it was as if she were being guided by something in her head. Suddenly, looming out of the gloom, she was both relieved and surprised to find herself back at *Honeysuckle Cottage.*

She found her mother sitting quietly in the parlour just staring into a large cosy fire. Without stopping she rushed over to her and held onto her tightly.

"Why Emily, what's the matter?" her mother said. "You're shaking and white as a sheet."

As Emily told her what had just happened, Mrs Williams became very alarmed and, cuddling her, she warned that Emily was never to go to the vault again. "The cemetery can be a frightening place" she said "and it can play strange tricks on your mind so perhaps it's not a good idea to go out in the fog or at night." As she comforted Emily she tried to treat the incident as simple imagination but in her own mind she knew there was more to it than that.

Chapter 17

A Warning from Clara

When Emily woke up the following morning she was pleased to see that the fog had lifted and the sun was shining again although there were some dark clouds on the horizon. What a difference it made and she quickly forgot about her frightening experience. Everything she had seen could be explained, just as her mother had said. Jim had probably disturbed the skeleton so it was ready to fall and the door had been freshly oiled so it could easily swing shut on its own. As for the voices, well, that was almost becoming normal.

Emily was pleased to see Madge at breakfast. She always brightened up the morning with her chatter. As they ate, Emily remembered what Tom had said about school holidays and decided this would be a good opportunity to raise the matter.

"So you want a holiday" her mother said as she buttered another slice of bread.

"Yes please Mother. Tom will be on holiday and it would be unfair if I had to work while he was having fun".

Mrs Williams looked at Madge and winked. "What do you think?"

Madge pretended to look serious and asked "Have you been working hard Emily and learned all your lessons?"

"Yes I have, honestly. Tell her Mother".

Mrs Williams and Madge both laughed and it was agreed that Emily would be given time off school for as long as Tom was off.

Emily was very pleased and, when the meal was finished, asked if she might be excused as she had something to do. Her mother looked apprehensive.

"You know you had a bad experience yesterday."

"Yes Mother but it wasn't real was it and anyway the sun is shining today."

Her mother finally agreed but told her to be very careful and to come home straight away if she got frightened.

Emily quickly helped to clear away the breakfast things and rushed out of the door with her mother standing, watching her go. She was still worried and Madge noticed her concern.

"What is it dear" she said.

Mrs Williams thought for a moment and, realising she needed to talk to someone about it, she asked Madge to sit down and told her all about Emily's special gift.

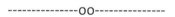

While heading towards the hill Emily had felt a little guilty about not including Tom but now, as she climbed up the steep slope, she knew that this was something she had to try. The sun was still shining, giving her confidence to be there on her own but she noticed that the dark clouds were now hurrying towards them on the freshening breeze. She quietly pushed her way through the bushes and stepped into the clearing. There, sitting on the little wall was Clara.

Clara looked just the same, pale complexion, dressed in white and with a distant look on her face but when she saw Emily she smiled slightly and, putting her head to one side as she did before, said "I'm glad you came."

Emily went over to the wall. "I hoped I would see you too" she said.

They immediately began chatting to each other like old friends. Clara didn't contribute much but avidly listened to Emily telling her all about her latest adventures. When Emily mentioned her odd experience at the vault, however, Clara's face suddenly turned very serious. She looked Emily in the eyes and warned her, "There are some dangerous things in this cemetery Emily and you need to be very careful where you go."

Emily thought for a moment and said "Do you think it was a ghost in the vault Clara, or just my imagination?"

Clara just smiled. "Perhaps you have a guardian angel watching over you."

Emily was intrigued by this suggestion but then quietly said "I hope my guardian angel is watching out for my father too." Clara listened as Emily told her about the telegram and the news that her father was buried in the mine. Clara listened sympathetically but then, looking directly at Emily, she emphatically said "He isn't dead."

It was a consolation for Emily to hear but it was strange the way Clara had said it, not just comforting words but almost as if she knew.

There were so many things Emily still wanted to know about Clara but she was still struggling to learn anything because of her odd, indirect answers.

"Tell me where you really live?"

Clara thought for a moment and gave her usual evasive reply.

"I used to live in London with my mum and dad. We lived in the East End but there was a terrible outbreak of cholera and everyone in the area became sick so we were brought here."

Emily was pleased that Clara was finally talking about herself but quickly realised that she hadn't actually answered her question.

"So you live close by then, is it far?"

All Clara said in reply was "No, not far at all."

Emily decided to change the subject "I was going to ask if you would like to come to my house some time to play. We could play with my doll or do some painting and you could meet my friend Tom."

Clara smiled. "It would be nice to come to your house and play with you but I don't think I should like to meet anyone else."

She stopped and looked directly into Emily's eyes.

"I like you. You are very special, did you know that? You have a very special gift and you can see things that other people can't see."

Emily was surprised by the comment and wasn't sure what it meant but before she could say anything Clara asked "Do you ever hear voices in your head?"

Emily was startled. "How did you know that?" she said, but Clara just stared. Eventually Emily admitted that she did but added that she didn't listen to them anymore or even tell anyone about them.

"The voices usually come in my dreams at night and people say it's just my imagination or a nightmare."

"Yes" said Clara, knowingly "they would say that." Then she added enigmatically "The voices are stronger at night and travel further. You should listen to them. It's important that you do listen to them."

Emily was surprised at the strange direction that the conversation was taking but, just then, she heard a voice in the distance calling to her. It was Tom shouting.

"Emily, where are you?"

Clara shifted uncomfortably and jumped down off the wall. "It's time for you to go" she said. "Look at the clouds, it's going to rain".

Emily was disappointed but, looking up, she saw that the heavy black clouds had arrived overhead and she could feel the first raindrops beginning to fall.

"What about you" she said.

"I will be fine" was the reply. "I like the rain."

Emily hurried down from the hill and immediately bumped into her faithful friend Tom.

"There you are" he said "Put this on quickly." He had brought a coat for her saying "Your mum told me where you were headed and I worried because I could see the rain clouds coming."

Emily was very grateful to her friend and, after struggling into the coat, they both hurried home.

Chapter 18

Lessons in Painting

For several days Emily thought about her strange conversation with Clara but was still mystified by what she had meant. Clara had seemed so adamant about listening to the dreams, almost as if she knew something. Perhaps, Emily thought, she needed to think more carefully about these dreams in future and work out what meaning they really had.

She had experienced a number of dreams recently but they all had the same theme revolving around her crawling across rocks, along a black tunnel in almost total darkness. When she had looked up there was no sky, no stars, but everything was covered in dust and the air was stifling, making it difficult to breathe. She had been aware of other people around her too, their voices calling out but they echoed and were indistinct so there was the usual frustration of not being able to make out what they were saying. Having had the conversation with Clara, however, she now realised that the voices were important for some reason so she resolved to listen more carefully when she next had a dream. There had been no new dreams recently, however, and for the first time Emily realised that you can't simply make dreams happen, you have to wait until they decide to come.

While waiting, their spirits were lifted one day when Madge hurried over to the cottage and rushed in through the open front door.

"Goodness" said Mrs Williams. "I wasn't expecting you until tea time."

Madge sat herself down. She had obviously been hurrying and needed to recover her breath. Mrs Williams poured her a cup of tea and they sat while she took a long sip from the cup and several deep breaths.

"You won't believe what's just happened" she finally said. "While the funeral party was in the refreshment room just now, one of the gentlemen, a tall man he was, walked over to your pictures on the wall and studied them for a long time. Then he asked me if I knew who painted them and if he could buy one."

Mrs Williams was stunned. "You mean he wanted to buy one of my pictures?"

Madge went on. "Yes, and when I told him about you he asked if you would sell the sunset picture of the cemetery and how much you would want for it."

Mrs Williams sat back in her chair, amazed but obviously pleased.

"I never believed that anybody would want to own one, and I have no idea what he would pay for it."

Madge stood up. "Well I have to get back now because they will be coming back from the graveside soon, so what shall I tell him?"

Mrs Williams thought carefully and finally said "Do you think he would pay sixpence for it?" She thought the money would help their finances and would more than cover the cost of the paper and the paints she had used.

Madge paused and said "He looks very well off so I think you could probably ask for more than that."

Mrs Williams then had a flash of inspiration, although it was also something of a gamble. "Give it to him, and tell him to pay what he thinks it's worth."

"Right" said Madge and she rushed off.

Mrs Williams was quite bemused by the whole episode but Emily was far more excited.

"Your paintings are always so good Mother but imagine being paid for them. Perhaps you could sell some more and we would be rich."

"Don't get too excited, my darling. We don't know yet what he thinks the painting is worth."

About an hour later, they heard the Necropolis train puffing through the cemetery heading back to London and Emily went over to the door to watch it go. As she watched the carriages rumble past, swathed in smoke from the engine, she turned to her mother and said "It must be so sad for them to go and leave their loved ones here."

Mrs Williams turned away and gently lifting her handkerchief to her eyes she said "Yes, it's very sad, but they will never forget them."

It wasn't long before Madge reappeared at the door with a rather large smile on her face. Emily was too excited to wait and asked "Did he buy it?" Madge just smiled and beckoned to her as she went into the front parlour where Mrs Williams was reading a book. She looked up and waited as Madge clearly had something to get off her chest.

"He bought the picture" she said "and when I said he was to pay what he thought it was worth, he gave me this and asked if it was enough."

She passed a folded piece of paper to Mrs Williams and when Emily took a close look, she could see it was a 10 shilling note. Mrs Williams was shocked.

"He gave you all that?" she said in an unbelieving tone. "Surely not."

Madge couldn't restrain herself any longer and blurted out the rest of her story.

"He also asked if you would accept a private commission at the same price. Sadly he has just buried his sister but as a last memory of her he wondered if you would paint him a nice picture of the grave and its surroundings with a sunset in the background."

Mrs Williams laughed and said "Well that's no problem. Isn't it exciting. I shall make a start on it as soon as the memorial stone is put in place."

Madge was still bursting with news, however, and went on to say "I haven't finished yet" as she placed the gentleman's business card on the table.

"His name is Mr Brown and he owns an art gallery in London and he asked if you would like to lend him some pictures to put on display in an exhibition."

Mrs Williams sat there speechless but Emily jumped up and down with pleasure shouting "You're going to be famous Mother, you're going to be famous."

That night Emily went to bed very happy. She had become aware in recent weeks that the family had financial problems but she didn't know the details and simply assumed that it would only be a temporary situation. Whatever the reason, if Mother could make money selling her pictures that must surely help.

Chapter 19

Emily's Dream

Emily drifted off to sleep very quickly that night and, being tired, she slept very deeply. Then, around midnight, she became restless, tossing and turning until she began to wonder if she had woken up or was she still dreaming? She was in an underground chamber again and it was very difficult to breathe with only one candle burning some distance away throwing out a very weak light. In the shadows she could see men lying on the floor or propped up against the wall. The voices were there too, moaning and calling out but Emily struggled to hear what they were saying although at one point she thought she heard the number "7" mentioned. She listened more intently as the muffled voices came and went but then one voice came over louder than the others as if someone was summoning up more strength.

It said "Must go down to 7" and then again "Go down to 7, level 7" over and over again.

The message meant nothing to Emily and as the dream faded she realised that she was not dreaming at all and was now wide awake in bed, staring at the ceiling. She tried to make sense of it but it was meaningless. Eventually she decided to lie back and try to sleep again in the hope that the dream would come back but, although she quickly fell asleep, there were no more dreams and no more voices.

At breakfast the following day she thought she should mention the dream to Kate and her mother in the hope that they might be able to understand what it meant. With Madge bustling around in the background she described the underground scene in some detail and repeated what the voices had said, adding "and I have no idea what level 7 means." She thought that they would laugh but they didn't, they just looked at each other. Mrs

Williams had a deep respect for Emily's dreams and her gift of being able to see things that other people couldn't see.

Finally her mother said "Did your dream look anything like an underground mine?"

Emily thought back and said "It could have been. There were some tools, a hammer and some spades and a pickaxe lying in the dust."

Mrs Williams got up from the table and went over to a small bureau in the parlour to pick up Uncle John's telegram. She read it again and it confirmed what she thought. He had written that the rock fall had taken place deep down *on level 6* of the mine and that was where the rescue team were now digging.

She stared at Emily without speaking for a few moments, deep in thought, and then began to scribble a note, telling Emily to run and fetch Tom as quickly as possible. Madge looked mystified but called after her "Go to South Station Emily. Tom should be there helping his father today."

Mrs Williams thought very carefully about what she would write and by the time she had finished, Tom was already standing, breathless at the door. She gave him the note and some money and said "Tom, please run to the Post Office in the village and get them to send this telegram. Please hurry Tom, it's very important." Tom didn't wait to ask any questions and in seconds he was off, running along the path towards the village.

Mrs Williams sat down and put her arm around Emily. "Was that telegram about me" Emily asked, feeling rather confused. There was a pause as Mrs Williams thought for a moment but she just said "I have sent a telegram to Uncle John."

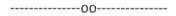

For the next two days Mrs Williams asked Emily each morning if there had been any more dreams but Emily had slept very well on both nights so there was nothing more to tell. In fact she had slept so well she hadn't even noticed if any night trains had come through. Life continued as normal although Emily noticed that Mrs Williams was on edge all the time and would often pace up and down the room as if she were waiting for something to happen. In the end she got her paints out and started painting her cemetery scene for Mr Brown in the hope it would help to calm her. It failed miserably and the resulting picture was a dark, autumnal scene with heavy, brooding clouds, bare trees, and piles of dead leaves on the ground being whipped up by a strong wind. It was a depressing picture. When Kate looked over her shoulder at it, she didn't say anything but Mrs Williams knew what she was thinking.

"This isn't what Mr Brown wants at all. It just reflects my mood so I will keep this one and paint him another when I am in a better frame of mind."

The following day, just as they were all about to sit down to tea, they heard the sound of a bicycle bell coming along the path. Mrs Williams rushed out the door just as the messenger boy pulled up at the gate.

"Telegram for you" he said.

She took it and quickly opening it, she carefully began to read. Emily and Kate watched her but she showed no emotion and just asked the boy to wait as she wanted to send a reply. She then hastily scribbled a new message, gave the boy some money and sent him on his way.

As she walked back into the house Kate couldn't contain herself

"What is it Mother?"

Mrs Williams sat down and looked at them both

"I'm not sure yet. It might be good news but we mustn't get our hopes up."

She didn't read out the telegram but just told them that in the earlier telegram she had sent to Uncle John she had asked if *level 7* meant anything to him and if there was any possibility that the men might be there. Uncle John was very surprised but when he investigated he found out from some of the older mine workers that there was indeed an old level 7 much deeper in the mine but it wasn't used any more as the tunnel had been blocked by a small rock fall many years ago and it wasn't worth clearing it as there was so little diamond bearing ore to be found at that level anyway. With the help of some of the miners Uncle John had found his way down to the old tunnel and when they reached the fall, they listened and heard tapping from the other side. Mrs Williams paused and then said "They think there are men in there, still alive, and the rescue team is now digging towards them on level 7."

Kate put her hand to her mouth and Emily gasped as they realised the implications. Madge, who had overheard all this from the kitchen, came and sat down beside them. They all sat in silence with their own thoughts until Mrs Williams was able to take a deep breath and continue.
"The thought is that there was gas building up on level 6 after the rock fall and to escape it the trapped men had somehow found a way down an old shaft leading to level 7. They don't know yet how many men may have survived or even if your father is amongst them."

Time seemed to stand still for the family as they sat there with just a glimmer of hope at last. Mrs Williams went off to her bedroom to be alone again and Madge, looking at the time, said "I must go and get the station ready now. You stay here Kate, I can manage both stations today as there is only one train due."

Kate stood up. "It's alright. I will come – it will help keep my mind occupied."

As they were leaving, Madge took a long look at Emily.

"Try to play quietly Emily, it would be best if your mother weren't disturbed for a while."

She then bent down close and, looking her in the eyes, said quietly "How did you know?"

Emily smiled weakly and just said "It was only a dream Madge."

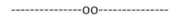

They all knew that it was more than just a dream, however, and over the next few days the messenger boy became a regular visitor to the cottage with a flurry of telegrams passing backwards and forwards between Mrs Williams and Uncle John. The latest telegram had arrived this morning, around 11 o' clock and it said that the rescuers were making good progress, despite having to prop up the roof to prevent further falls, and they hoped to break through to the chamber very soon. There was now a mixture of excitement and fear as everyone tried to continue as usual but the waiting was very frustrating and quite stressful.

Then, later in the day as Emily helped Madge and Kate tidy everything away at North Station, Mrs Williams burst into the refreshment room with another telegram in her hand and tears streaming down her cheeks. They all looked up as she said in a voice faltering with emotion "He's alive!"

Chapter 20

The Mine Accident Explained

Over the next few days the family were the happiest they had ever been and it felt as if a heavy weight had been removed from their shoulders. From what she was reading in more telegrams from Uncle John, Mrs Williams was still worried about her husband's health but she had been reassured that, despite his very poor condition, he would make a full recovery. She had even considered travelling to South Africa to be with him but Uncle John had been opposed to this saying that there was no point. It would take at least three weeks for her to sail there and Uncle John hoped that by then Mr Williams would have recovered sufficiently to already be on a boat heading home.

More information had now come to light regarding the accident. In fact, from his hospital bed, Mr Williams had given a statement to the police that it had been no accident and that his partner, Griffiths, had deliberately lured him down the mine and then set off an explosion using dynamite in order to kill him. The police were looking for Griffiths but he had disappeared when he heard that the miners had been brought out alive. The police had immediately searched his house and found a treasure trove of diamonds and money that he had stolen, all of which would now be returned to Mr Williams and the mining company. Further good news was that nobody had been killed in the explosion though many of the miners had been injured and had later suffered even more in the tunnel when the food ran out. As Mr Williams had known the mine so well, when the tunnel had begun to fill with poisonous gas, it was he who had been able to lead them all to a small shaft that connected to the lower, level 7 passage.

The news about their father was uppermost in the girls' minds but with the revelation that they would soon get all their money back, they began to discuss the possibility of moving back to London. Emily was adamant that she now liked their little cottage at Brookwood and although it was quite small, it was very cosy and peaceful and she would miss all her friends, especially Tom and Madge. Kate admitted that she felt the same and, without saying as much, was thinking how much she would miss Frank.

"Do you think we could just stay here?" asked Emily, but Kate thought it very unlikely.

"We can discuss that with mother at some point in the future but not now."

They already realised that Mr Williams' recovery would take several weeks and his journey home would take another three so they wouldn't be seeing him for some time. Life had to return to normal but it was now a much more cheerful environment. Mrs Williams wrote long letters to him and both girls added their own messages with Emily telling him all about her adventures at Brookwood. They also received some very cheerful letters from Mr Williams telling them how well he was feeling now and how the mine had recovered from its earlier financial problems.

Uncle John had been organising everything since Griffiths disappeared and he had become so interested in the work to the point that he was now enthusiastic about buying Mr Williams' shares in the mine. This would suit

Father as he still wanted to sell it and was planning to retire back to England and just enjoy spending all his time with his family. Interestingly he mentioned in one of his letters home that, while he was trapped underground, he had been in a semi-conscious state and had dreamed about the family on several occasions. In particular, he remembered thinking that he was at home talking to Emily.

Mrs Williams, now in a happier mood, also felt better prepared to paint Mr Brown's picture and, although the money was no longer an important issue, she wanted to do it for him and was still intrigued at the possibility of having her paintings exhibited in a gallery. She finished the painting in only two days and wrote to Mr Brown asking if he still wanted it. The reply came very quickly confirming his wish to buy it, even without seeing it, and he wondered if she would be prepared to travel up to London to see him, bringing all her paintings with her. Mrs Williams wasn't sure but Madge insisted she went.
"There's nothing you need to worry about here" she said "and it's still weeks before Mr Williams comes home. It's a wonderful idea. Why don't you take Emily with you for a day out?"

It was all arranged. Emily was excited at the prospect of the train ride and seeing London again, and making the journey in daytime would mean she could enjoy the views along the way, unlike her first journey down to Brookwood in the fog. The day before they left, Mrs Williams was packing her bag and carefully placing her paintings in a folder when there was a knock on the door. It was George. "Sorry to disturb you" he said "but I heard you needed to go to London tomorrow and I wondered if I could help. We have a number of specials running earlier and later than usual tomorrow. We are still doing the normal funeral parties at 11 o'clock and 2 o'clock but there will be an early morning special, carrying no passengers, which will be returning to London at 9 o'clock and it will do another run back here at 4 o'clock. I could put you on the train if it would help."

"Why that would be perfect Mr Robinson. Are you sure it would be no trouble?"

George smiled. He liked the way she always called him Mr Robinson as it showed respect.

"No trouble at all" he said with a broad smile. "It will be Frank and Edward doing the run so I will let them know."

Chapter 21

A Journey to London

The following day the special arrived very early and the new batch of coffins were unloaded by the gravediggers while Frank filled the engine boiler tanks with water. Mrs Williams and Emily arrived on the platform in good time and George showed them into one of the empty passenger carriages. Emily was very excited and studied the inside of the carriage as her mother thanked George. "Thank you again Mr Robinson, this was very kind of you."

George nodded and said "Have a good trip" as he closed the door.

As Emily settled down on the comfortable seats, they heard a whistle outside and almost immediately the train gently started to move out of North Station, this time the engine pushing the carriages from the back, towards the main line at Brookwood station. The train went very slowly and they both enjoyed the view of the cemetery, bright and colourful in the morning sun. There was no need to use the passing loop but they had to wait for a train to pass on the main line before the signalman allowed the driver to push out onto the down line and then pull back across to the up line. The train then slowly ran through Brookwood station and, as it left the platform behind, it began to pick up speed. Emily was thoroughly enjoying the experience, looking at the fields and villages as they passed, and crossing the occasional river. She rushed from one side of the carriage to the other, looking out of both windows so as not to miss anything. Mrs Williams had pulled out a book from her bag and just sat there quietly but was pleased that Emily was enjoying the journey.

It seemed like no time at all before the train was entering the outer suburbs of London and the countryside gave way to houses and factories, packed into grubby streets all sitting under a pall of dark smoke. It made them both realise how much nicer it was living in the country. For a while, the railway line ran alongside the River Thames and Emily could see large ships loading at the wharves and tugs struggling to pull barges against the flow of the current. It was all very exciting.

The train finally began to slow as it jerked and clattered over some points and drew into the London Necropolis station. As Mrs Williams was gathering up her bag and portfolio with the pictures in, the door was opened for them by their train guard, Mr Evans. He helped them down onto the platform and, in an unmistakable Welsh accent said "Now don't forget Mrs Williams, that we will be leaving here for our last trip back to Brookwood at 4 o'clock". He looked down the platform and, seeing the stationmaster hurrying towards them, he added "Now there's lovely, Mr Dawkins is wanting to speak to you."

Mr Dawkins arrived, obviously out of breath, and smiled at Emily before saying "Hello Mrs Williams, I just wondered if you would like to join me in my office for a cup of tea if you have time?"

Mrs Williams thanked him and, looking at her watch said "We are a little early so that would be very nice."

They walked down the platform together and as they passed the engine they could see Frank and Edward busily working in the cab as the engine gave off clouds of steam. Frank looked up and Emily called out "Thank you for giving us such a nice ride Frank."

Edward, the driver, laughed and jokingly called back "He didn't do much miss, he just shovelled the coal."

Frank pretended to be offended and poked Edward before calling out "See you later Emily."

Mr Dawkins' office was just as cosy as Emily remembered and they were soon sitting down enjoying their hot drinks. He told them how pleased he had been to hear the news from South Africa, so clearly Emily's Uncle John had been in touch with him. He was also interested to hear how they had been getting on at Brookwood and was pleased that they had settled in so well. He told them that the station staff had been very busy at the Necropolis owing to the cholera epidemic and people were still dying of it in the east end of London.

"As you've probably seen at the cemetery, we've had to run many specials recently to take all the bodies but the situation seems to be improving now so I suspect they are getting it under control. It's all to do with the water you know." He then stopped and, looking very serious, said "Now don't you go anywhere near that East End while you are here in London."

Mrs Williams assured him they wouldn't and, looking at her watch said that it was time they left for their first appointment. As she thanked him he said "I will be here all day so if you need a rest or a cup of tea, just drop in, but please be sure to be back by 4 o clock."

Outside the station, Mrs Williams hailed a cab and the driver quickly carried them to the art gallery in Covent Garden. Emily couldn't believe how busy the streets were and found it very noisy. Although this was all interesting and exciting, she was beginning to miss Brookwood already.

The art gallery was a large, imposing building with a wide flight of steps leading up to the front door. As they walked into the lobby Emily was immediately impressed by the size of the room with its high walls covered in paintings and a domed glass roof providing bright, natural lighting. A lady sitting at a desk looked up and asked if she could help. Mrs Williams explained that they had an appointment with Mr Brown whereupon the lady quickly jumped up and, after introducing herself as Mr Brown's secretary, escorted them down a corridor marked in several places with signs reading *PRIVATE* in big letters. She showed them into a large office in which there were three gentlemen deep in conversation, around a desk. One of them, sitting behind the desk, was

Mr Brown and they all stood up as Mrs Williams and Emily were shown in.

"Mrs Williams to see you sir and …. I'm sorry, I didn't catch the young lady's name."

Emily looked at the secretary and, despite being a bit shy, thought she should be polite. Turning to the three gentlemen she announced "I'm Emily and I'm very pleased to meet you."

All three smiled and one stifled a chuckle as Mr Brown walked around the desk and warmly shook Mrs Williams' hand. "Thank you so much for coming" he said. "It's such a pleasure to meet you at last." He then introduced his colleagues who were both sponsors of the gallery.

"I hope you had a pleasant journey" one of them said as Mr Brown spoke to his secretary, asking her to bring in some tea for them all and some lemonade for Emily.

"Mr Brown has told us about your beautiful paintings and we are very anxious to see them. We hope you managed to bring some?"

Emily wasn't particularly interested in the conversation that followed but visibly brightened when her lemonade arrived. She walked over to a big window at the back of the office and stared at the busy street scene with cabs, wagons and horse drawn buses everywhere. It brought home to her that the atmosphere and way of life that she had now become used to at Brookwood was so different from this. Life in London was very busy and so impersonal with little time for meaningful friendships.

She turned and looked around the room and immediately noticed a picture on one of the walls. She recognised it as the one that her mother had painted and which Mr Brown had bought when he had visited the cemetery. It was beautifully framed and she thought how lovely it was that he now had it hanging on his wall.

Opening her portfolio, Mrs Williams first carefully removed a folder in which was the painting that Mr Brown had commissioned.

"I do hope you like it, but, if it's not what you want please say so."

There was a nervous silence as Mr Brown opened the folder and looked at the painting. He stared at it for a long time, taking in the perfect perspective, the beautiful colours and the fine detail.

He finally looked up at Mrs Williams and said "It's wonderful Mrs Williams. It's even better than I had hoped for, and such a beautiful memory of my late sister's final resting place and its lovely surroundings. Thank you so much."

Mrs Williams was pleased that he liked it but felt very embarrassed when he mentioned payment.

"No Mr Brown, I enjoyed painting the picture so please accept it as a gift. You have already paid me enough with the first picture you purchased."

Mr Brown didn't press the point but was clearly pleased and impressed with Mrs Williams' kindness, saying that he would always treasure the picture. He then asked if they could now see the other pictures and she passed a second folder to him.

The three gentlemen gathered round the desk and spent the next half hour going through the paintings, their admiration for Mrs Williams work being obvious from their complimentary comments. One of the sponsors said "You clearly have great artistic talent, Mrs Williams - the pictures are an amazing collection and we have rarely been so impressed by a new and unknown artist."

Mrs Williams felt herself blush as the other sponsor added "Would you be prepared to leave these with us so we can exhibit them as a collection?"

Emily was by now listening with great interest. This was such an opportunity, she thought, and it could make her mother famous. She was pleased when Mrs Williams agreed and was even more excited when she heard that visitors to the gallery would often offer to buy exhibits on display.

"Would you be prepared to sell any of them?" the gentleman asked. Mrs Williams said she would but would let the gallery decide on the value of each painting.

Having finished making the arrangements, Emily and Mrs Williams were treated to a guided tour of the gallery, each section devoted to a specific artist or a specific subject or theme. Mrs Williams was overwhelmed by the quality of the exhibits, many by famous artists, and she still found it hard to believe that her pictures would soon be hanging alongside them. Mr Brown even showed her the blank wall where her pictures were to be displayed. When the tour was finished, they were invited to lunch at a rather expensive hotel across the street where the food and service was excellent. The whole experience made Emily feel very important.

Chapter 22

An Unusual Train Journey

After they had taken their leave of Mr Brown and his colleagues, Mrs Williams told Emily that she had to visit their bank manager and also call in to see the private detective that they had employed but, seeing that Emily was now looking quite tired, she suggested that she could take Emily to the station first and leave her in the care of Mr Dawkins. Emily was very happy with that idea and half an hour later she found herself sitting by the fire in Mr Dawkins' office, drinking warm milk while he sat behind his desk, working his way through a large pile of documents. He talked to Emily as he worked, asking her about her new life in the country. She had lots to tell him and the time passed very quickly.

Emily was just washing her glass in a little sink in the corner of the office when the door opened and Driver Sykes walked in.

"We're back" he said in a gruff voice. "This afternoon's funeral party have just left the train and O'Hare is loading some more coal so it's ready for the freight run at 4 o'clock."

Sykes always described the runs carrying just coffins and no passengers as *freight runs* which Mr Dawkins thought was very disrespectful.

"Very well, I'll sign you off duty now." With that Sykes left the office without another word or even acknowledging Emily's presence.

Emily sat down again and, looking at Mr Dawkins, innocently said "Mr Sykes must be a very careful driver Mr Dawkins."

He looked up from his papers and with a questioning look asked "What makes you say that Emily?"

Emily thought for a moment and said "When I'm in bed I can hear the night trains running through the cemetery. I hear them whistle when they reverse back from Brookwood station and I hear them go past our cottage. When Frank and his driver are doing the night run it only takes 5 minutes to get through the cemetery but when Mr Sykes is driving it sometimes takes him nearly half an hour to get to our cottage. He must drive very slowly"

She carried on playing with her doll but Mr Dawkins sat back in his chair and became very thoughtful.

"Are you sure, Emily, or do you think you might be mistaken or perhaps have fallen asleep?"

"Oh no, Mr Dawkins, it happens a lot and I have even timed it using the clock when I am awake."

Mr Dawkins was puzzled and said no more but sat thinking for a long time.

Not long afterwards Frank and Edward looked into the office.

"Just starting our shift Mr Dawkins. Hello Emily, you're a bit early. We won't be leaving for a little while yet I'm afraid."

She smiled and said "It's okay Frank. Mother left me here while she went to some other appointments."

Frank beamed. "Well that's perfect" he said. "Would you like to come and have a look at the engine? You could climb into the cab and have a good look at all the controls, if that's okay with you Mr Dawkins?"

Emily jumped up with excitement and said enthusiastically "Ooh, yes please Frank."

Frank looked at Mr Dawkins who nodded his head slowly but added "You be very careful with our young lady here Frank. She has been left in my safe care and I don't want anything to happen to her."

"Will do Mr Dawkins" and then they were gone, Emily skipping along beside Frank as they walked up the ramp to the platform.

When they arrived at the engine, Edward pointed to a large number on the side of the cab.

"This engine is officially number 30025" he said, "but we just call her *Belle* which sounds much nicer. She's such a beautiful engine, what they call an M7 class. Just look at all those polished levers and dials. Every engine has its own different number so they don't get mixed up."

He then helped her up onto the cab platform, which he explained was called the footplate, and began to show her all the controls. There were knobs, dials, gauges, pipes and levers everywhere and it all looked very complicated, even a little frightening with the hissing noises coming from the boiler and the occasional blast of steam. Edward showed her the coal bunker at the back of the cab which held the coal for the fire and opened the door of the firebox below the controls in which a fire was raging. There was a lot of heat coming from the open door and Frank began shovelling more coal into it.

"I've shown Tom how this all works several times" said Frank "and I reckon he knows enough to drive her now." Edward then let her pull the whistle lever down and there was a piercing, high pitched scream as the whistle echoed around the station.

She was still enjoying her time in the cab when her mother arrived with Mr Dawkins.

"Mr Dawkins said you were up here" she said. "I hope you haven't been a nuisance?"

Edward raised his cap. "Hello Mrs Williams" he said, and laughing he added "She's been no trouble. We've been teaching Emily how to be our relief driver."

Emily reached up and said "Look what I can do Mother" as she pulled the whistle lever down again. Mrs Williams jumped back at the noise and, when she had recovered said "That's quite enough of that young lady! Come along"

Frank and Edward were having serious conversation in the cab as Emily climbed down onto the platform and Mr Dawkins escorted them to their carriage and helped them in.

"It was lovely seeing you again Mrs Williams, and you Emily." Then, looking at Emily, he said "Perhaps I will see you again soon" and winked.

Mrs Williams thanked him for all his help and Emily gave him a big smile, saying "Thank you for my milk too."

They both settled down in the carriage as Mr Dawkins went back to his office.

"It has been a very successful day Emily. The bank manager has now had all the recovered money transferred into our account and the detective has given me all the information we need to prove that Griffiths had been forging the letters that your father was supposed to have written. I don't think we have any problems now" and she smiled. "I hope you enjoyed your day as well?"

"Yes I did Mother, and I'm so pleased that the gallery is going to exhibit your paintings. You will be famous."

Mrs Williams laughed but just as she was going to reply, there was a gentle knock on the carriage door and it was opened by Frank.

"Excuse me Mrs Williams" he said as he leaned in and quietly whispered something to her. Mrs Williams looked at Frank in surprise, eyes wide.

"Is it safe?" she said. "I'm sure she would love to but would it be all right with everyone?"

Emily was puzzled and asked "What is it Mother?"

Mrs Williams turned to her and said "Frank and Edward wondered if you would like to ride in the engine cab on the journey home?"

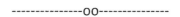

----------------oo----------------

As the train pulled out of the Necropolis station, Edward told Emily to crouch down out of sight until they were past the signal box but once they were out on the main line she was able to stand up and enjoy the experience fully. She had to hold on tight but there was a much better view from here than in the carriage and the feeling of speed was far greater with the wind on her face and her hair blowing around under her bonnet. It was truly exhilarating as she watched the houses and fields rushing past. The smoke frequently blew into the cab, occasionally making her cough, and she sometimes had to stand to one side as Frank shovelled more coal into the firebox. He even let her shovel some coal in herself but the shovel was very heavy and she could only lift a small piece of coal at a time. As they approached a level crossing Emily was pleased when Edward asked her to sound the whistle to warn people that they were coming. From then on it became her job to sound the whistle every time they approached a station or a level crossing. It was great fun and an experience she would never forget.

When they arrived back at North Station Mrs Williams walked along the platform to collect her from the cab but Emily was already running along the platform towards her with a big grin on her face. "Mother, it was amazing, and did you hear the train whistle? That was me." Mrs Williams pretended to look shocked and said "Look at the state of you Emily, your hair is all over the place and there's soot on your face. I'll have to get you home and give you a good wash before anyone sees you." Emily knew when her mother was joking and, continuing to smile as she turned round and waved to Frank and Edward who had followed her along the platform.

"All safe and sound" said Edward. "She was really helpful on the way back."

"Thank you so much," said Mrs Williams. "That was very kind of you."

Chapter 23

A Visitor in the Night

It seemed no time at all before another telegram arrived from Uncle John with more good news. Mr Williams had recovered sufficiently and was already on his way home on a fast ship which was due to arrive at Liverpool docks about a week later. This was wonderful news and Mrs Williams became very excited and immediately made plans to travel north. She wanted to be there to meet him and bring him home and decided to travel early and stay with an aunt who lived in Chester, only 20 miles from the Liverpool docks. It would be a good opportunity to visit her aunt whom she hadn't seen for several years and, while staying there, she could make all the local preparations for her husband's nursing care and the journey south.

Although it would mean leaving the family at Brookwood, Mrs Williams was happy that Emily would be well looked after by Kate and that they would both be under Madge's watchful eye. The telegram had arrived on Wednesday and by the following Monday Mrs Williams had said goodbye to Emily and Kate and she was on her way north.

Later that week, as Emily lay sleeping in bed, the voices returned. It was a quiet, background noise like before, just lots of whispered conversations taking place at the same time but all of the voices indistinct and difficult to hear. They sounded sad and monotonous like a constant droning noise but they didn't disturb her until suddenly a much louder voice quite clearly called "Emily." She immediately woke up. "Was that a dream or did someone just call me?" she thought as she lay there in the darkness. She waited, all her senses on edge as she listened, and then it came again. "Emily". This time she sat up, suddenly frightened and heart pounding. She looked around her room but she could see by the light of the moon shining through the window that there was nobody there and Kate was still asleep. The background voices had faded away and she sat there, scared and listening in the silence for any further sounds. Just as she thought she had imagined it the voice came again.

"Emily, come to the window."

She hesitated at first, wanting to just pull the covers over her head but curiosity overcame her fear and she very bravely got out of bed and crept over to the window. As she peered out she could see a full moon over the cemetery making everything bright and clear but there was a thick mist drifting around at ground level. The moonlight reflecting off the damp tombs creating mysterious, long dark shadows. In the distance she thought she could see faint white shapes moving between the gravestones, or was it just the mist. They appeared to effortlessly drift across the paths, in and out of the shadows but they were so indistinct it could have been just imagination.

The voice suddenly called again and Emily looked down. To her horror there, standing at the garden gate, was a motionless white figure with its back to her. The figure didn't move at first but then slowly began to turn around and although Emily, remembering the skeleton, was terrified of what its face might look like, she couldn't take her eyes off it. The figure continued to turn, very slowly, and then stopped and looked up at her. It was Clara.

Emily hesitated, frozen to the spot, but then Clara's voice came to her again.

"Emily, I've come to speak to you."

This was all so strange. Emily slowly opened the window, feeling the cold night air on her face and whispered "What are you doing here?"

Clara's face looked pained and she replied "You said I could come and visit you."

"Yes, but not in the middle of the night. Everyone's asleep."

Clara's face was expressionless. "It's important" she said. "I want to show you something."

Emily closed the window and, after slipping on her shoes and a coat over her nightdress, and making sure Kate was asleep, she tiptoed downstairs. She opened the door but quickly jumped back, startled to find Clara, now standing on the doorstep staring at her.

"Did I frighten you" she asked in a voice that showed no emotion.

"A little bit" replied Emily "but it's all right now. What did you want to show me?"

"You will have to come with me".

There was something about the way she said it that Emily didn't like but she simply said "Where to?"

Clara turned and walked down the path but then stopped and, looking back over her shoulder said "Don't be afraid Emily, as long as you are with me you will be quite safe." She waited as Emily thought this over.

"I'm not sure" she said. "Can't I come and see it in daylight?"

Clara just stared at her but finally she very quietly said "Trust me" and in that moment Emily knew she had to.

Emily picked up the lantern which was kept by the front door but, seeing that the moon was so bright, she didn't need to light it but took it anyway as she followed Clara down the path and they set out across the cemetery in the direction of the hill. Emily kept her head down and didn't look too closely into the dark shadows although she was still conscious of the moving shapes and ethereal figures around them, seemingly watching them. As they walked, Emily became aware of the moon reflecting off Clara's white dress, almost as if it was glowing. She hadn't noticed it before but her hair and face seemed to be glowing too, and even her hands and feet. In fact, although Clara was walking, she was so light on her feet that they didn't even seem to touch the ground but just danced over it. Emily thought it must be some strange trick of the moonlight but it continued to disturb her.

"Where are we going" asked Emily, beginning to worry about being so far into the cemetery, so late at night. "Kate might wake up and worry."

Clara didn't stop walking but said rather ominously "She won't wake up" and then added "It's not far now."

They reached the base of the hill which Clara, without slowing down, seemed to glide up effortlessly while Emily, encumbered by her nightdress and thick, heavy coat, struggled to reach the top. They then pushed their way through the trees and bushes which now completely blotted out the moonlight and Emily could only see where she was going by following Clara's white dress. Eventually they reached the open clearing which lay in a pool of moonlight in front of them. Clara led her over to the shaft and as they got nearer, Emily could hear a strange, disturbing hissing noise coming from it.

"We have to go down there" said Clara looking over the edge of the wall.

Emily was shocked. "You want me to climb down there" she said, not as a question but in sheer disbelief. She looked into the shaft and could hear the hissing, much louder now, and she could see light at the bottom of the shaft. "No, I won't do it, it's dangerous" she said "and I'm scared."

Clara looked disappointed, and Emily thought she might be about to cry.

"I know you are scared Emily and I understand that, but as long as you are with me I promise I will keep you safe. This is very important to me and you are the only person who can help me. Please come."

Emily sensed a change in Clara's manner. Whereas before she had been calm and confident, she now sounded desperate and Emily felt sorry for her. She only knew that her friend was in trouble so, without thinking too deeply about the danger, she said "Very well, I will."

Clara's face brightened and she stood close to Emily and said very quietly "Thank you."

Chapter 24

A Mystery Explained

Clara climbed over the wall and, easily lifting the grille up on her own, she began to climb down the ladder. Emily watched her and then, deciding that there seemed to be enough light coming up the shaft, she put her lantern on the grass, felt for the ladder, and then followed Clara down. It wasn't an easy climb and the ladder was cold and wet. The walls of the shaft were brick lined but they were old and, by the glow of light coming from below, Emily could see that most were covered in thick green moss. She looked down, surprised to see so much light below her and realised that most of it seemed to be coming from Clara, even though the moon was no longer shining on her. The hissing noise which had been constantly in the background got louder the deeper they went. Emily's heart was pumping with a mixture of fear and excitement but she pressed on until, quite suddenly, she realised she was at the bottom of the ladder.

She looked around and saw they were in a short, dark tunnel that led into a larger chamber beyond which was illuminated by a flickering light. Clara caught her eye and put her finger to her lips indicating that Emily must be quiet and say nothing. She then crept forward to the opening which looked out into the chamber and as Emily peered over Clara's shoulder, her eyes widened.

The chamber was dimly lit by candles that reflected weakly off the black, rock walls which were dripping with water. Loose rocks were scattered over the floor and to the left, the chamber entered a tunnel which disappeared into darkness while to the right the chamber stopped against a solid rock face. Running through the centre of the chamber was a railway track which came to a dead end at the rock face but the aspect that most amazed Emily was that standing on the track was a Necropolis train. A mixture of steam and smoke from the chimney was swirling around the engine, deflected downwards by the low roof, reducing visibility and making the air very smoky. The engine hissed continuously and the cab was eerily lit by a bright red glow from the firebox. This was totally unexpected and Emily tried to take it all in, wondering what was going on.

As she stared, she became aware of movement further down the train and of shadows walking to and from the carriages carrying something large and heavy. It was difficult to see but a sudden gust of air cleared the smoke and for an instant Emily caught sight of Driver Sykes and O'Hare removing a box from one of the Hearse Carriages. "Oh" she cried in a shocked voice but Clara immediately swung round and put her finger to her lips again. Emily ducked down but fortunately they hadn't heard her over the noise of the engine. The men began loading several more boxes back into the train and then Emily heard the sound of doors being closed.

"Have you finished yet" an impatient voice called out from the back of the train but Sykes ignored it and climbed back into the cab of the engine followed by O'Hare. Emily then saw the guard putting out all the candles and, holding a lantern up high, he climbed onto the back of the train as it slowly reversed back down the track and disappeared into the darkness.

Now that the tunnel was deserted, leaving only the heavy smoke, they walked out onto the train track which was only dimly lit by the strange, faint glow appearing to come from Clara. There was so much that Emily didn't understand and her mind was in a whirl but she didn't say anything and just watched as Clara walked over to one of the candles and lit it with a match that was lying alongside the candleholder. The tunnel was illuminated again by the dim light from it but Emily remained silent, suspicion growing in her mind as she watched Clara put down the match and turn back towards her. They just looked at each other for what seemed a long time but eventually Emily summoned up the courage to ask the question that was now foremost in her mind.

"Clara, who are you?"

Clara's reply was evasive. "I'm your friend" but that wasn't good enough now and Emily only hesitated before asking "Are you a ghost?"

Clara put her head to one side as if she was thinking and said "I prefer to think of myself as a spirit."

It was confirmation at last. Emily felt a cold chill run down her spine and she began to slowly move backwards. Seeing the look of horror on her face, Clara quickly took a step forwards

"Please don't be afraid Emily, I am not going to hurt you. I'm what you would call a friendly spirit, not like some around here that you have already met in that vault. I have been looking out for you ever since I realised that you could see me. Most people are unable to see or hear me so I am very lonely down here and quite sad. At least I can talk to you with your special gift and I want to ask you for your help Emily."

This all seemed so unreal and Emily was beginning to think that she was still having some kind of dream. Yes, that would explain it. She had been in bed so this was just a dream which would explain why she hadn't felt frightened until now. She continued the conversation, hoping she would wake up at any moment.

"How can I possibly help you Clara? Tell me, why are you here, and what was the train doing in the tunnel?"

Clara beckoned to her and led her over to a large pile of rocks that had fallen from the roof.

"Be careful Emily, the roof is very unstable and there are lots of rock falls in here."

She pointed to the bottom of the rock pile and Emily could just see the end of a box, like one of the coffins, sticking out.

Clara's voice became very sad as she said "This is where I live."

Emily sat down on a large rock on the tunnel floor.

"I don't understand" she said. "Please explain it all to me Clara."

"The train crew you saw tonight are all very bad men. The reason they like to make the night runs on the train is that it allows them to do bad things under cover of darkness."

Emily was intrigued. "What bad things." she asked.

Clara paused before continuing as if she was trying to remember something and then said in a rush "Yes, that's it, they steal bodies - I think you call them *Resurrection Men* or *Bodysnatchers*."

Emily was horrified. "Why would they do that?" she asked.

"It's because bodies can be sold for a lot of money to doctors and medical organisations." Said Clara. "The doctors practise on them and learn by cutting them up."

Emily was even more horrified and said so.

"That's disgusting. Is that why they were moving the boxes?"

Clara nodded. "On the night runs into the cemetery they quickly bring the train into this tunnel, remove some of the bodies, fill the empty coffins with rocks and then put them back on the train. It doesn't take long and, because the dead are poor people and there are no mourners, there's nobody to notice or even care that anything has happened."

At this point Emily's head was spinning. Whether it was the bad air, the darkness or this incredible story she didn't know but she felt she needed to get out of the tunnel quickly. There was still a question on her mind, however, that she had to ask before she could leave.

"Why is it that you live here?" she said pointing to the half-buried coffin.

Clara sat and looked up at the roof. "When they first brought me here, they unloaded my coffin but before they could take the lid off there was a rock fall which almost completely buried me. It was too dangerous for them to move the rocks in case the whole roof came down so they just left me here."

Clara looked as if she was about to cry when she said "Emily, please help me. I want to be taken out of this horrible tunnel and buried properly in the cemetery, next to my mother and father."

Chapter 25

Emily's Ghost Story

Emily woke up in her bedroom with the sun streaming through the window. She sat up and looked around. Everything looked normal. She lay back again and thought about the strange dream she had. It had seemed so real and thinking back on it she realised how scary it had been. In fact, it had been so odd that it must have been a dream. As she lay there she heard Kate calling from downstairs. "Are you up yet Emily? Your breakfast is nearly ready."

Emily quickly jumped out of bed and hurried over to the washstand to wash her face. As she picked up the jug of water she suddenly noticed how dirty her hands were. She was puzzled. "How did that happen" she thought. She washed and dressed and went downstairs to breakfast. Madge was busily organising some bacon in the kitchen so Emily made a start on the toast.

"You were up late this morning" she said. "Didn't you sleep well?"

Emily giggled and said "I had the strangest dream Madge, you wouldn't believe how scary it was."

Madge put a large plate of bacon and sausages down on the table but looked concerned. "Before your mother left she warned me that you might have some bad dreams so you must tell me if they bother you. Anyway, it's a lovely sunny day now so you just try and forget all about it."

Emily helped herself to a slice of bread and spread some butter on it. "It's all right Madge, it was only a dream."

They continued to eat but then, as Kate poured herself another cup of tea, she casually said something that made Emily drop her knife.

"Emily, do you know where the lantern went? I'm sure it was by the front door when we went to bed last night."

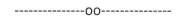

Emily was deep in thought as she helped to clear away the breakfast things.

"Madge, where is Tom today?"

Madge was busily cleaning the hob and looked up. "He's helping his dad with something over at South Station" she said "but it shouldn't take him long. Why don't you go over and find him."

"Thank you Madge" she said but then she added "There's something I have to go and do first though" and then she looked at Kate to see if she would let her go.

Kate smiled and said "Go on then" so with a big grin, Emily picked up Lizzie who had been sitting at the table with them and rushed out the door.

She headed straight for the hill and in no time she was climbing up the slope. She had done it so many times now that she knew every handhold and foothold and was soon at the top, pushing her way through the bushes. The ventilation shaft came into view and she slowly walked forward and then stopped. There, lying in the long grass at the base of the little wall was the lantern, where she had left it. So she had been here last night. It wasn't a dream after all.

Emily made her way to the station deep in thought, calling in at the cottage on the way and carefully placing the lantern by the door where it normally stayed. As there was no-one around, there was no need to explain and she hurried off again heading for South Station. She found Tom working in a large flower bed at the back of the platform. There were lots of cheerfully coloured flowers growing but George had said there were too many weeds growing too so he had set Tom to work clearing them out. He was bored but he cheered up when Emily arrived.

"Tom" she said. "I need to speak to you and it's very important."

He stopped and looked up at her. "This is going to take me all morning" he said "so perhaps we could talk about it this afternoon."

Emily thought for a moment and then got down on her hands and knees. It was very unlike her but in a very determined voice she said "No Tom, it needs to be now. I will help you to weed the flower bed and I will tell you all about it as we work."

Over the next hour Emily told Tom the whole story of her dream. George occasionally walked past and was pleased to see them both intently working together and obviously locked in conversation but several times he noticed Tom stop and look up at Emily with an expression of disbelief on his face. "Mmm" he chuckled to himself "must be a serious conversation."

By the time Emily had finished her story, the weeding was finished and Tom sat back and looked at her. He was going to laugh but when he saw the expression on Emily's face he stopped himself.

"You do realise how daft that story sounds" he said. "I can't believe you're serious, and as for Clara, the ghost that no-one except you has ever seen or heard. Well, I ask you!"

"I know Tom, but it all seemed so real and I'm sure now that I did go to the hill last night but I need to know for certain. I must go down that ventilation shaft to see if the rest of it was true. I know I have to go down there but please say that you will come with me."

Later that day they were sitting in Emily's kitchen eating the tea which Kate had prepared for them. They talked quietly as they discussed their plans while Kate was busy in the kitchen.

"Dad tells me there are some more night runs tonight." whispered Tom. "The trains have been kept very busy this past week because there is a backlog of bodies to be buried as a result of the cholera outbreak. Most of them now are from poor families so there are no mourners travelling with them which is why so many are coming at night".

They decided that they would go to the hill when everyone was in bed. Tom promised that he would make his way to Emily's house shortly after dark and throw a pebble up at her window when he got there. He wasn't happy about going against his father's orders but he also felt a loyalty to his best friend. Anyway, they would just take a quick look so it wouldn't take long. Tom looked Emily up and down and said "You're about the same size as me. I'll bring some of my old clothes for you to wear. Trousers would be far more practical for climbing than those big dresses girls have to wear."
Emily looked shocked. "What me! You expect me to wear trousers?"

Chapter 26

The Tunnel at Night

That night Emily went to bed early but she couldn't sleep and she was still awake when Kate came to bed. Fortunately Kate only read her book for ten minutes before she blew out the candle and settled down. Emily was still hoping that Tom wouldn't just fall asleep or forget to come and she was also worried that if he threw a pebble at the window it might wake Kate as well. She decided it would be safer if she got up now and waited downstairs. She quietly got out of bed and slipped her dressing gown on. Kate was sleeping soundly and seemed unlikely to wake but, just in case, Emily tucked her pillow under the covers so that to a casual glance it would seem as if she was still in bed.

Emily gathered up Lizzie and quietly tiptoed down the stairs in total darkness, feeling her way as she went. She decided it would be unwise to light the lantern and went over to the door instead and opened it slightly to let the moonlight in. The moon was hidden behind a large cloud bank, however, making the cemetery dark and uninviting and she was not sure that she would now be able to see Tom coming. At least the night was warm so she opened the door fully and sat down in the doorway. Almost immediately there was a rustling in the bushes beyond the fence and a fox slowly stepped out and silently walked across the garden. She was still watching it making its furtive way back into the bushes when she heard a train whistle. It was the first of the Necropolis trains running that night, reversing into the cemetery from Brookwood station. She listened intently and noticed, rather oddly, that it didn't seem to slow when it reached the run around loop but then it went very quiet. It took a very long time, far too long in fact, but eventually it appeared in the distance, slowly coming around the curve, partially hidden by the trees. The cab was giving out a ghostly orange glow from the firebox.

"That's strange" thought Emily. The engine was pushing the carriages back which it wasn't allowed to do. It drew nearer and, although it was quite dark, Emily withdrew into the house as it passed in case the train crew saw her. Reflected in the light of the firebox she could see it was Sykes driving the engine tonight.

The train rumbled on towards North Station and she stepped outside to watch it slowly come to a standstill at the platform. A sudden movement in a bush at the end of the garden made her jump and she thought at first it was the fox returned but to her relief she realised it was Tom.

"That was lucky" he said in a low voice. "I was following the track when the train came and I had to jump off and hide in the bushes until it had gone past. Did you see that? The driver hadn't bothered with the run-around loop and was just pushing the carriages through the cemetery."

"I'm glad you came" whispered Emily as Tom handed her some clothes and said "Here, put these on" and then, as an afterthought "and what are you doing downstairs, I thought I would have to wake you?"

Emily went into the cottage while Tom waited outside. She slipped the trousers and an old coat he had brought over her nightdress, and he had even brought an old pair of sturdy boots that were just the right size. She stood up and thought how strange it felt. "How on earth can boys stay comfortable wearing these things all day" she thought to herself.

She went back outside where Tom was patiently waiting. She expected him to laugh when he saw her but he didn't. He just said "That's far more practical." As it was so dark Emily took the lantern again before they set off across the cemetery but she waited until they were over the railway track before she lit it. In the distance, they could hear the sounds of coffins being unloaded at the station but as they hurried towards the hill, only whispering to each other, Emily could see by the weak light the lantern threw out that a ground mist was forming again and it was getting thicker the nearer they got to the hill. Eventually they struggled up the slope and Emily had to admit to herself that climbing was so much easier in trousers. She still felt self-conscious about her strange appearance but it was dark so at least no-one else could see her.

They stopped at the entrance to the ventilation shaft and, holding the lantern high, they looked down it.

"It's very dark" Tom said. "Are you really sure you want to do this?" He thought for a moment and said "If you want to stay here, I could go down and look for whatever it is you want to see."

Emily was touched by his kind gesture but insisted that she must see for herself. They lifted the grille and, with Tom leading the way and holding the lantern with some difficulty, they began to slowly climb down the ladder. Tom stopped several times trying to reposition the lantern as it was difficult only having one hand to climb with but eventually they reached the bottom. Emily took the lantern and led the way into the tunnel.

When Tom saw it he was speechless and just stared at the scene.

"It's amazing" he said at last, his voice echoing around the empty chamber. He quickly took in the black, damp walls, the broken timbers that had once supported the crumbling roof, muddy puddles spreading across the floor, a few abandoned empty coffins and four strange, ominously familiar shapes wrapped in shrouds lying by the wall. He walked over and looked closely at the railway lines and could see from the light reflected off them that they weren't rusty but quite shiny and obviously used recently. Emily joined him and reminded him not to touch anything as the roof was very unsafe.

"Is this how you remembered it from your dream?" he asked.

"Yes" said Emily "Exactly, and look over here." She held the lantern up and walked over to the rock fall. There, sticking out from the pile of rocks was the battered end of a coffin. Emily looked at it with sorrow in her eyes and whispered "This is where Clara is."

They stared at the coffin for some time, each with their own thoughts, but they were suddenly jolted out of their contemplation by a loud squealing noise down the tunnel. They both looked in horror, fearful of what might appear when they heard the rumbling of a train coming into the tunnel.

"That was the tunnel gate opening and the Necropolis train is coming" said Emily in alarm. "Sykes is bringing the train in here again."

Tom looked around and, just before the train emerged from the darkness, he spotted a small pile of rocks and so he quickly doused the lantern, saying urgently "Come on Emily, hide behind here."

They had just ducked down when the train rumbled past and stopped alongside them, the engine hissing loudly. The guard was holding a lamp up and he quickly jumped down and walked along the train to meet O'Hare and Sykes who had now climbed down from the engine.

"I wonder what they are going to do?" whispered Emily.

"Hurry up" shouted the guard as he opened the doors to one of the Hearse Carriages. "We don't want to keep old Foxy waiting."

"Who's Foxy" whispered Tom, but Emily just shrugged. Their eyes were now becoming used to the darkness and they saw Sykes and O'Hare walk over to the four, shrouded shapes on the floor and between them lifted one up and carried it back to the Hearse Carriage and pushed it inside. They then repeated this until all four were loaded.   Tom quickly realised what they were seeing.

"They are bodies" he gasped. "They are stealing bodies, just like Clara told you!"

"But where are they taking those bodies now?" whispered Emily.

"I don't know" said Tom "but this is serious and we need to report it to the police straight away."

Just then, O'Hare walked towards the pile of rocks where Tom and Emily were hiding.

"This rock pile is getting low" he said. "I think I'll just stack a few more on the heap before we go so they will be ready for the next run."

Emily looked at Tom in horror. "He's coming over here" she whispered. He would certainly see them but, just as Tom was wondering what they could do, O'Hare said "I'll just check the money first." He walked to the blank wall at the end of the tunnel where the railway track finished and, lifting up a large rock, he pulled out a bag and started counting its contents. The train guard followed him saying "Stop wasting time, O'Hare, the money is still there where we left it" but Sykes was clearly irritated by the delay and walked over to the engine and climbed into the cab.

"Quick" said Tom "we have to move now."

They crept out from behind the rock pile while the others had their backs turned and ran over to the train where Tom quickly ducked under the Hearse Carriage with the open door. Emily hesitated for a moment before following him but she wasn't happy climbing between the big wheels and crouching between the tracks. The train seemed so big from underneath and she was terrified that the train might start moving. Her fears suddenly became reality when the train shuddered and the engine gave a long blast of steam.

"Come on" shouted Sykes. "I'm going now, with or without you."

"We can't stay here" said Tom. "They're about to move off."

They climbed back out from under the carriage but, hearing O'Hare running back along the train again, Tom said "Quick, in here" and they clambered up into the open Hearse Carriage. No sooner had they hidden behind the coffin racks when O'Hare slammed the door as he ran past and a moment later the train began to move off into the tunnel. Emily looked at Tom, her eyes wide.

"Where are we going?" she asked, but she already guessed the answer. The train was on its way back to London.

Chapter 27

An Unexpected Journey

"Don't worry" said Tom as the train rolled through the tunnel. "They'll probably stop when they get outside and we can jump down then." Their hopes were dashed, however, when the train slowly eased out of the tunnel and, despite the ground mist that still persisted, the clouds had cleared and the cemetery was now bathed in bright moonlight. Instead of stopping, the train continued to move forward slowly while the guard hopped off, closed the tunnel gate, and then ran after the train and climbed back on. The train then quickly picked up speed heading for Brookwood station.

"What are we going to do?" said Emily. "We can't go to London, we are both supposed to be in bed and we will get into such a lot of trouble."

Tom thought carefully and suddenly remembered that the train was pulling the carriages towards Brookwood so it would need to use the run-around loop to change ends before the journey back. Sure enough the train came to a standstill but just as they were about to open the carriage door they saw the guard slowly walking to the other end of the train on one side of the carriage while the engine was running past on the other side. There was no opportunity to leave the carriage unnoticed, particularly as the sky was now completely clear and the moon was so bright.

After O'Hare recoupled the engine, the train pushed out onto the mainline and, after a brief pause while the Brookwood signalman changed the points, the train pulled back, crossed over to the up line and slowly rolled through the station before picking up speed again heading for London.

"Well that's it" said Tom in a matter of fact voice, "we're going to London."

---------------oOo---------------

They sat there in darkness, the carriage interior being illuminated only by the moonlight shining through the window and reflecting off the four shrouded bodies on the floor. Emily couldn't believe what was happening. Only about an hour earlier she had been in her comfortable bed but now, with Kate fast asleep at home, here she was on a train heading for London and in all sorts of trouble. She eventually broke the silence and asked "What shall we do Tom?"

There was no immediate response from him as he was deep in thought but Tom was a very practical person and slowly an idea came to him.

"It's not a problem" he said, "so don't worry. Dad said that there were to be two night runs tonight so once this train gets to London and loads up with more coffins, it will head back to Brookwood again. If we keep our heads down and no-one spots us, I'm sure we could sneak off the train when it gets back to the station and we could be back in bed in a couple of hours."

Emily was encouraged by this. Tom then went on. "I've been thinking and I reckon I can see what the train crew are doing now. I'm sorry I didn't believe you but it's exactly as Clara described it to you. When the night run comes down to Brookwood with a new load of coffins the crew must quickly run the train into the tunnel and unload some of them, remove the bodies from the coffins, fill the empty coffins with rocks instead and then deliver them to the station for burial. No-one would ever know!"

"Yes, it all makes sense now" said Emily "but we still don't know what they do with the bodies?"

"Well we just saw that" said Tom. "They leave the bodies in the tunnel out of sight and pick them up on the way back, probably removing anything valuable that may have been put on the body for its burial, and then they take them to whoever buys them."

"I bet that's this Foxy person" said Emily.

Tom thought for a moment and said "Yes, you're right. Perhaps we'll see where the bodies finally go, but it must be difficult unloading them at the Necropolis station at Waterloo as there would be so many people about, even at night."

They then reverted to silence again with Emily sitting on one of the coffin racks and Tom standing by the window watching the fields roll by in the moonlight. What he couldn't see but Emily was very aware of, was a faint white mist forming around the four bodies lying on the floor. It had not been noticeable at the start of the journey but as time slipped by the mist was getting thicker and was starting to form into shapes. Emily was now becoming worried again and chose not to look at them.

All at once they heard a loud whistle from the engine up ahead and almost immediately they felt the train beginning to slow down, just coasting slowly for a short distance before coming to a complete standstill.

"This is unusual" thought Tom. "The run to London has no scheduled stops so the signals must be against them for some reason."

He looked out the window and saw up ahead a signal but it was showing *clear* so there was no reason to stop. He lifted his head higher and, looking down, he saw that they had stopped on a high embankment leading over a road bridge and below them, on the road, he could see a wagon and horses with two men dressed in dark clothes waiting by it. Tom was suddenly aware of voices coming from outside and heard the guard shouting from the back of the train

"Hurry up, we have a clear signal and we can't stop here for long."

Hearing running footsteps on the gravel outside Tom quickly turned to Emily and gestured for her to hide behind the coffin racks. He had just joined her when the door was flung open and Sykes and O'Hare reached in and started pulling the bodies out of the carriage, none too carefully. When all four were on the embankment, O'Hare slammed the carriage door shut and they began to carry one of the bodies down the slope to the wagon. Tom crept back to the window and beckoned for Emily to join him.

"Keep your head low" he said "but look at this."

Emily carefully peered over the window ledge and saw that all four men were now carrying the bodies down the slope and loading them into the back of the wagon. This was all done quickly and in silence but when they finished, an argument broke out between Sykes and one of the other men. The moonlight was throwing long shadows across the figures and Emily thought how wicked this new man looked. He had removed his hat and she could see he had a thin face, very little hair and a sharply pointed nose on which was balanced a pair of spectacles. Their voices became louder and Emily heard Sykes shout "Come on Foxy, I want the money now."

So this was the mysterious Foxy who was buying the bodies. The second man told Sykes to calm down and said "Get on your way Sykes before anyone spots us. Dr Fox will pay you next time."

"So that proves it" whispered Tom. "He's a doctor!"

Just then the guard began shouting at them again.

"Come on" he shouted impatiently. "The signalman up ahead will be getting suspicious, and if we're not quick we'll be getting a fast express into the back of us."

That settled it. With Sykes refusing to budge, Dr Fox hurriedly pulled out a small wallet and practically threw some money at Sykes before climbing up on the cart as his partner began to drive it away under the bridge. Sykes and O'Hare turned and were quickly climbing up the embankment causing Tom and Emily to crouch lower in the carriage. They rushed forward to the engine and immediately started the train again towards London.

Chapter 28

Panic at Necropolis Station

Emily pulled Lizzie out of her coat and sat cuddling her. What an adventure this was turning out to be. Tom was beside himself with excitement and couldn't sit still, pacing backwards and forwards across the carriage.

"We have the whole story now" he said. "We will be able to tell the police everything, and they might even be able to catch them in the act. What a pity they couldn't be at Brookwood waiting for them tonight. There are lots of policemen in London but we only have two at the police station in Brookwood village and they're both quite old." With that thought, Emily had an idea. "Why don't we report it in London and they will know what to do. We can tell Mr Dawkins at the Necropolis Station and I'm sure he would sort it out. After all, the railway is his responsibility."

Tom was impressed with the idea.

With Sykes making up for lost time, the train hurried through the outer suburbs of London and was soon approaching Waterloo station where it branched off to the right onto the small siding leading into the Necropolis station platforms. As the train stopped, Emily and Tom carefully peered out of the window. The platform was quite dark but they could see two porters talking by a wall and another wheeling a trolley along the platform. Sykes called out to them as he climbed down from the cab.

"Get them loaded quickly. We're off for a cup of tea and we'll be leaving for Brookwood in half an hour so make sure you're finished by then."

With that the train crew walked down the platform to their little rest room. The porters turned and one of them whispered "Bossy so and so isn't he." The porters then opened a wide pair of tastefully decorated, polished doors which hid the storage room where the coffins were kept. There were several storage rooms at the station to ensure that the various coffins of different religions were kept out of sight from any daytime funeral parties. The porters stepped inside and busily began loading coffins onto trolleys.

"Quick" said Tom. "Now's our chance to see your Mr Dawkins." Instead of getting out onto the platform, however, he opened the carriage door on the other side. "We will have to go this way" he said "so we won't be seen."

He climbed down onto the railway track between the platforms and turned to help Emily down behind him. Then, keeping low, they ran along the track to the front of the train where the engine was standing. Emily recognised that it was *Belle* and she was surprised how big it looked from ground level and the hissing from the steam pipes made it quite frightening. Tom checked that it was all clear and then helped Emily up onto the station platform where they both ran as fast as they could to the ramp leading down to the station entrance, half expecting to hear voices shouting after them. They felt relieved that they hadn't been spotted and Emily felt even better when they finally turned the corner at the bottom of the ramp and saw the lights of Mr Dawkins' office.

Emily led the way into the little room but, as she looked around, she was dismayed to see that Mr Dawkins wasn't there.

"Where is he?" asked Tom in a worried voice.

"I don't know" said Emily. "He must be off around the station somewhere."

Tom wasn't sure what to do next. "We haven't got time to go and find him" he said. "The train will be leaving soon and we need to be on it."

Emily had an idea and looked around. "There" she said spotting paper and an inkwell on Mr Dawkins' desk. "We can leave a message for him."

Tom looked down at the floor and clearly felt uncomfortable. "I'm not good with my letters" he said, "could you write it?"

Emily could see he was embarrassed and quickly said "Of course I will Tom, after all Mr Dawkins knows me."

She sat down and, finding a quill pen on a tray, she dipped it in the inkwell and began writing to Mr Dawkins explaining everything that they had seen and politely asking him to do whatever he thought best. Tom was watching the big clock on the wall and getting impatient. "Nearly finished" said Emily and finally added to the message "We are getting back on the train now ... your friend, Emily."

With the letter left in a prominent position on the desk, they both rushed out and hurried up the ramp to the platform, careful to stay in the shadows to avoid being seen. They reached the top of the ramp and as they cautiously stepped onto the platform, they froze in horror. The train was gone.

"We've missed it" said Emily despairingly but Tom quickly reassured her.

"No," he said. "They've just used another engine to move the carriages into the other platform. That way, our engine can get out and re-join the front of the train. Come on" and he led the way around to the second platform which fortunately was in complete darkness. They quickly moved along the platform but when they were halfway along the train they heard voices behind them. It was the train crew returning.

"Hurry" said Tom as they ran towards one of the first class carriages and he quickly opened the door and pushed Emily inside. "That was close" he said. "I think we just made it in time."

They both hid on the floor but as Emily bent down a sudden thought crossed her mind. She felt inside her coat and was horrified.

"Lizzie's gone" she said in a loud voice.

Tom instantly put his hand across her mouth and whispered "Shhh, Emily, be quiet" but Emily was distraught.

"Lizzie is precious Tom, I must find her."

"You must have dropped her on the platform" he hissed and he slowly lifted his head to look out the window. Sure enough, there was Lizzie lying in full view on the platform. Anyone walking past would see her and would wonder how she got there or might even be suspicious enough to search the carriages. He slightly opened the door and looked down the platform. Sykes and O'Hare were talking to Parker and there was clearly an argument taking place. The platform was still dark so, while the train crew were occupied he crept out, leaving the door ajar, and dashed across the platform, grabbing the doll as he ran past and dropping down to hide behind some crates. He listened, but the arguing continued as before so he realised he had got away with it. He was just about to dash back when the voices stopped and he heard heavy footsteps walking along the platform towards him. He didn't dare reveal himself and just waited as Sykes and O'Hare walked past, still complaining. O'Hare suddenly stopped. "Look, those porters have even left this door open" he grumbled and he slammed it shut before moving on towards the engine. Emily jumped with the sudden noise of the slamming door but stayed hidden on the floor. She was now getting very worried about Tom and began to wonder if he was going to be able to get back on the train. Tom was also getting worried. He watched as the driver and fireman reached the engine and climbed up into the cab but just as he pressed Lizzie into his coat pocket and prepared himself for the dash back to the carriage, he glanced back down to the rear of the train and saw Parker, standing on the platform, looking towards the engine, waiting for a signal from the crew. There was now no chance of crossing the platform unseen.

After a few moments there was a loud blast of steam from the engine, quickly followed by a short whistle and Sykes leaned out the cab and waved to Parker. The guard checked his watch and then waved his green flag. Almost immediately the train shuddered and the carriages rattled together as the engine pulled forward and took up the slack in the couplings. The train slowly began to move and Tom saw Emily's horrified face looking out of the carriage window, her eyes wide. Tom looked back down the platform but Parker was still there. The train was picking up speed and as the last carriage passed Parker, he reached out and expertly took hold of the last door handle and stepped up into the open doorway. The train was going faster now and, after taking a final glance along the length of the train, Parker stepped into his carriage and slammed the door.

Tom knew this was his last chance. In seconds he was on his feet, racing along the platform in the hope of leaping onto the train but it was already getting faster and, even though he was a fast runner, it was beginning to outpace him. He ran faster still, heart pounding, but realised he was losing the race. Then, just as he was about to give up, the carriage door opened and Emily held her hand out shouting "Come on Tom." He made a last desperate spurt and grabbed her hand but he could feel his legs giving out and he had no energy left to jump. "It's no good" he thought but at that moment Emily gave a great heave and he felt himself fly through the air and tumble through the door on top of her. He lay there, exhausted and gasping for breath but thankfully Emily had the presence of mind to get up and go to the open door. The station was now far behind them and the trackside was rushing past at a frightening speed. She held on to the doorframe and reached out, grasping the handle of the door while the wind rushed past, blowing hair into her face and forcing her to close her eyes. For a brief moment a thought flashed through her mind. "What would Mother say if she could see me doing this?" She gave the door a long pull and finally managed to slam it shut.

She sat down, still shaking from the experience silently watching Tom as he lay on the floor, slowly recovering -

his breath becoming less laboured. Finally he said "Thank you" and, reaching inside his coat, he pulled out Lizzie and held her up to Emily. Her eyes went wide and she gave a cry of delight as she took the doll and cuddled it. "Oh thank you Tom" she said, adding "You don't know how much she means to me." They smiled at each other and for the first time that evening they both relaxed.

Chapter 29

A Desperate Message

Mr Dawkins returned to his office shortly after the children had left but he went straight over to the fire and, following a well-practised routine, he prodded the fire with a poker and placed another lump of coal on it. He had been making the final arrangements for the following day's funerals and had gone to speak to the Waterloo station master to check on the express and special train times that the Necropolis trains would have to avoid. He had just turned back to his desk and sat down when he noticed the message Emily had left. It was written neatly but seemed to be in a child's hand which completely baffled him but after reading the first few lines he was astonished.

"So that's what Sykes has been up to" he said out loud.

He read on and the further he read, the more his eyes widened. It was a very detailed account of some very serious criminal activities. If this was all true, he thought, the train crew would all be going to prison. He eventually came to the end of the message and his mind suddenly whirled when he saw Emily's signature.

"Emily!" he said. Then he re-read the last line.

"We are getting back on the train now … your friend, Emily."

Mr Dawkins was horrified. "They mustn't risk getting on the train again" he shouted as he leapt up and ran for the door.

His mind was racing as he ran up the long ramp in his attempt to stop the train but he arrived at the platform just in time to see the last carriage disappearing into the darkness. He stood there, watching and wondering what to do next.

"You okay Mr Dawkins?" a voice said, obviously concerned at his odd arrival in such an agitated state. It was one of the porters.

"I have to stop the train" Mr Dawkins said, and then asked "Did you see any children get on it?"

The porter was surprised but said that he hadn't seen anyone get on except the train crew. Suddenly an idea came into Mr Dawkins head and without another word he started running towards the end of the platform. The porter scratched his head and, turning to his colleague, he said "You don't think he's going to run after the train all the way to Brookwood do you?"

Mr Dawkins reached the end of the platform but kept running down the short slope onto the railway tracks and, carefully checking that there were no trains coming, he ran across the six sets of tracks towards the Waterloo signal box. He had to wait at one point as a long passenger train loomed out of the darkness, slowly heading into the station. He had seen the remains of people run down by trains and it wasn't a pretty sight. He might be in a hurry but he was in no mood to end up like that. When the train had passed, he ran on to the signal box and climbed the stairs into the control room which was full of levers for setting the points and signals along the tracks. There were two signalmen on duty, both of whom he recognised.

"Hello Mr Dawkins, we don't often see you here."

Mr Dawkins had no time for idle chatter and blurted out "Has the Necropolis passed the distant signal yet?"

The signalman, hearing the urgency in his voice, quickly checked the levers and said "Yes, just cleared and is over the points and onto the main line now."

Mr Dawkins had guessed as much but it had been worth a try.

"Is there a problem?" the signalman asked, fearing that there may be a train accident about to happen but Mr Dawkins simply said "I need you to act now. Can you use your Electric Telegraph to send an urgent message to the Brookwood signal box" and he began to dictate the message.

Tom and Emily watched the moonlit countryside roll past as the train steamed towards Brookwood. There seemed to be no urgency now and they were unaware of the measures Mr Dawkins was undertaking to ensure they would be in no further danger.

"We must be getting near the station by now" said Tom. "It's been quite a night for excitement and I'm looking forward to getting home and into bed."

Emily laughed. She too was feeling more relaxed now and, like Tom, she was now hopeful that she could get back to bed before anyone noticed she was missing. The signed message she left at the Necropolis station might take some explaining though.

The train slowed as it approached Brookwood station and the children crouched down so they would be out of sight to anyone watching from the platform. Although it was night, there was usually a stationmaster and porter on duty somewhere. Sykes was in a hurry, however, and instead of stopping at the platform he rolled forward and stopped in the holding area on the main line, waiting for the signalman to change the points for him. The signalman had become occupied translating an urgent message from London, however, and was only interrupted when Sykes gave an impatient blast on the whistle. He stood up and pulled a large lever changing the points and then set the signal to *clear* allowing Sykes to reverse into the cemetery. He then went back to the message.

He had been used to using the old telegraph system which read out the letters directly but this was the recently introduced Morse telegraph system which used a sequence of dots and dashes to represent letters. Although it would be faster eventually, he was not an expert and had to keep referring to his book to check what the letters meant. He got up again as soon as Sykes had reversed onto the cemetery track and changed the points again, setting the clear signal for the main line as the night mail express was due in half an hour. Before he sat down again he noticed that Sykes hadn't stopped to use the run-around loop and was pushing the train backwards through the cemetery which was strictly against rules. "He'll get caught doing that one day" he said to himself as he returned to the message.

As the train pushed back through the cemetery it slowed almost to a standstill and Parker jumped off the rear carriage and ran to the points lever, quickly throwing it over. The train slowly rolled onto the old track leading to the tunnel, giving the guard enough time to run forward and unlock the gate. The children were surprised to feel the train lurch sharply as it turned onto the tunnel track but became really alarmed when they heard the familiar squeal of the tunnel gate as Parker opened it. He climbed back onto the last carriage and waved to Sykes indicating the way was clear before the train rolled slowly into the tunnel and total darkness.

Chapter 30

Terror in the Tunnel

Emily and Tom looked out the carriage window in dismay as the bright moonlight suddenly disappeared leaving them in total darkness. Tom reached out in the dark and held her hand.

"Don't worry" he said, "it will be all right if we just stay quiet."

The train wheels squealed as the train went deeper into the tunnel, the track curving slightly as it went. They still crouched low but Emily couldn't resist taking a quick look over the window ledge. The engine, pushing from behind, was throwing a vivid red glow from the firebox across the tunnel walls and Emily could see the eerie shadows of the driver and fireman reflected off the walls as they moved around in the cab.

Tom joined her at the window and, as their eyes continued to get accustomed to the dark, they saw that they had arrived in the wider chamber at the end of the tunnel and felt the train come to a standstill. Sykes stayed in the cab but, even before the engine stopped, O'Hare had leapt down and was running along the train to the hearse carriages where he met Parker coming from the other end of the train. The children heard him shout "Foxy asked for two more this time so let's be quick" Parker quickly opened the door and they pulled out two coffins which they prised open and removed the bodies, placing them carefully by the tunnel wall. They then went to the rock pile and brought rocks to put in the coffins before nailing them down again and replacing them in the carriage.

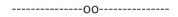

Back at the signal box, the signalman had translated the message and was amazed by what it said. He wasn't allowed to leave the box unattended so he rushed out onto the signal box balcony and shouted for the stationmaster who quickly appeared from his office.

"Quick," shouted the signalman, "urgent message, come and read this."

The stationmaster hurried over, crossing the tracks and climbing up the stairs where the message was thrust into his hand. He read it, eyes widening, and asked "Has the Necropolis gone into the cemetery already?" The signalman nodded his head whereupon the stationmaster said "Don't let it back out" and rushed back to his office. He found one of the two porters on duty and told him to run to the police station immediately to bring the police and if they weren't there he was to go to their houses and rouse them. He then turned to the other porter who had just arrived and told him to go and fetch George immediately. "This involves Tom so he needs to know" he said.

---------------oo---------------

It was clear that O'Hare and Parker had now finished their work and were preparing to leave.

"Time for us to go" whispered Tom. "If we climb down on the other side of the carriage we can probably creep over to the ventilation shaft and climb up it."

Emily nodded and Tom cautiously opened the door a little to look out. There wasn't much light but there was just enough to see the dark shadow on the back wall which was the opening leading to the shaft. There was no-one in sight. "Come on" he whispered "let's go."

He jumped from the carriage and helped Emily down but just as they began to move towards the shaft, O'Hare walked around the rear of the train carrying a lantern and spotted them.

"Hey" he shouted. "What are you doing here?"

The children froze but O'Hare ran forward and grabbed Tom by the arm. Tom struggled and shouted "Run Emily" but she wasn't going to leave him.

O'Hare roughly pushed them towards the engine and ordered them to climb up into the cab where Sykes was bent over the firebox with a shovel in his hand. He turned as he stood up, his face showing shock more than surprise.

"What's all this" he said aggressively.

"I found them skulking around in the tunnel" growled O'Hare, "and I think they were in the train."

"What did you see?" shouted Sykes, his eyes blazing.

Parker arrived alongside the engine, wondering what all the shouting was about, just as Sykes repeated the question.

"We saw everything" said Tom defiantly "and we know all about the bodies you have been stealing."

Sykes glared at him, but before he could say any more Emily added "and we've told the police so you're all going to be arrested."

Parker and O'Hare looked at each other. "The game's up, Sykes" said Parker. "We need to get out of here now."

"No!" hissed Sykes. "I can take care of these two and we can sell them to Foxy."

Parker was horrified and he said "I'm not having any part in that Sykes, dead bodies is one thing but this ..." He left the sentence unfinished. "I'm going to get my money and then I'm going" and with that he ran to the back of the train and started looking for the rock hiding their money.

"Get after him" Sykes growled "while I take care of these two kids."

O'Hare jumped down and ran after Parker. He found him on his hands and knees behind the last carriage pulling the money bag out of its hiding place under the end wall of the tunnel chamber. O'Hare shouted "Give that here" and jumped on him and the two men began to fight on the track.

In the cab Sykes was looking menacing and he advanced on the children as they backed up to the coal bunker.

"If you harm us, that will be murder and you will really be in trouble then" said Tom bravely. Sykes laughed as he raised the shovel above his head and was about to lunge at them when he froze as a large, dark shadow passed over the cab. Sykes looked up, surprised, and when he looked down again there was a large black shape, looming over them, seemingly rising up from the coal bunker on the back of the engine. Sykes watched as its shape swirled and changed until, by the glow of the firebox, he could make out a giant bird, sitting on the coal, glaring at him with wicked red eyes. Its beak was hooked and its large claws were sharp, glinting in the firelight.

Sykes was still holding the shovel above his head but, with a faltering voice, he only managed to croak "What the ...." before the bird launched itself at him. With one flap of its giant wings it was on him, talons sinking deep into his chest while the wicked, hooked beak slashed at his face. Sykes screamed and staggered back, dropping the shovel as he tried to fight off the bird. The weight of the bird forced him down, all the while slashing at his face and body with its beak and talons. The pain was unbearable and as he fell Sykes instinctively reached out to grab something to hold on to. His hands made contact with the engine regulator and, as he grasped it to pull himself up, the regulator moved down, opening the steam valve and applying full power to the engine. The engine instantly jerked and pushed backwards.

At the rear of the train O'Hare was still wrestling with Parker on the track but he finally knocked Parker down and grabbed the money bag from him. Parker was lying across the tracks, unable to move and only half conscious as O'Hare stood up, smiling to himself. He turned to walk back along the track but froze as his brain tried to take in what was happening. The back of the train was rushing towards him. His mouth opened in horror and he hopelessly put his hand up in a vain attempt to protect himself but neither he nor Parker could move in time and just stared with eyes wide. In a matter of seconds the train crashed into the rock face at high speed, crushing O'Hare against the wall as the carriage splintered and its metal frame and wheels rose up into the air. But the engine hadn't finished yet and kept pushing so the next carriage shattered and derailed, scattering more fragments of wood and metal across the scene. The force of the crash brought rocks tumbling down from the roof, slowly at first but then increasing as they started to bury the remains of the carriages. Suddenly there was an ear splitting roar and the entire section of tunnel roof collapsed, bringing tons of rocks down on the shattered remains of the last two carriages, completely burying them and the bodies of O'Hare and Parker.

Chapter 31

Escape into Danger

The impact of the train hitting the wall had been felt in the cab where Emily and Tom were thrown off their feet. Tom found himself falling from the cab onto the chamber floor while Emily struck her head on the coal bunker which stunned her and she collapsed onto the footplate. The bird had left Sykes and was standing over her, guarding her as Sykes recovered and stood up but the crunching and grinding sounds of the splintering carriages could still be heard over the noise of the falling rocks as the engine continued to push back. Despite his pain Sykes realised what he had done and, wiping blood from his eyes, he threw the engine reverse lever to the forward position but he knew it was already too late to save the rear of the train or the train crew. He whirled round, his eyes mad with anger, and glared at Emily lying on the floor but he wasn't going to tackle her with the bird standing over her so he jumped down from the train to where Tom was just getting up, still winded from his fall. The wheels of the engine were now spinning in the other direction, full ahead, but the engine was held captive by the buried carriages and the wheels just squealed on the track while the couplings strained and creaked.

Sykes was a mess, his face and body covered in blood from his injuries, his clothes ripped and torn, and he looked like some evil monster as he stood over Tom, his face red by the glow of the firebox.

"You caused all this" he screamed and picked up a large rock as Tom backed towards the tunnel entrance. Sykes lunged forward but Tom was too quick for him and stepped further back towards the tunnel, noticing that Sykes was now limping and dragging one leg. Tom couldn't see Emily but quickly had the idea of luring Sykes further into the tunnel to get him away from her. He turned and pretended to be injured as he hobbled into the darkness of the tunnel. He could hear Sykes heavy breathing and cursing following behind him but didn't look back. It was pitch black but he could feel the track under his feet which helped to guide him and at last he saw a faint glow at the far end of the tunnel which he guessed was moonlight shining into the tunnel entrance.

He tripped over a rock on the track and fell down but quickly picked himself up and risked a look back over his shoulder. In an instant he took in a scene which he would never forget. The lamp that O'Hare had been carrying had been smashed in the rock fall and the oil spilling from it was now ablaze at the other end of the chamber. The splintered wooden carriages had become a raging fire giving off clouds of black smoke which were quickly filling the chamber with choking fumes. It was like a scene from hell. Outlined against this backdrop was the silhouette of Sykes limping after him along the track but what grabbed his attention was the bird, flying into the tunnel behind Sykes and sweeping down on him. There was no time to waste and Tom began to run again but he had only taken a few steps when he heard a scream from behind him. At that same instant there was a squeal and grinding noise from the engine as the couplings on the rear carriages finally snapped with the enormous strain and the engine, no longer held back by the rock fall, leapt forward dragging the remaining carriages behind it. The last two of these were both on fire and had been derailed, the wheels now bouncing along the track bed ripping up the sleepers as they went.

The muffled sound of many voices had roused Emily back to consciousness. She had been lying stunned on the cab footplate but now she became aware of background voices in her head, a constant babble of noise that was unclear. Then one voice came to her, louder than the rest and more urgent.

"Emily, wake up Emily, you need to wake up. Please wake up"

She slowly opened her eyes and sat up but for a moment she couldn't understand where she was, and couldn't make out what the awful screeching was or the thick smoke and flames. She briefly glimpsed Tom running into the tunnel followed by Sykes, and - was that the buzzard flying into the tunnel behind them? She took in the frightening scene and it quickly became clear to her. Then came a grinding and snapping noise followed by a sudden jerk as the train had broken free and leapt forward. She stood up and looked out. There was no-one in sight now but the train was moving fast towards the tunnel entrance where she had last seen Tom. The cab was quickly enveloped in darkness as the engine entered the narrow tunnel, the only light being the red glow from the firebox. She instantly realised that Tom wouldn't see the train coming in the darkness. She had to warn him somehow and then she knew what to do. She reached up and grabbed the whistle lever, pulling it down and keeping it down to alert him.

Tom heard the whistle and instantly realised the train was coming. He increased his pace and prayed that he wouldn't trip again. He sensed the engine was getting closer and the screaming whistle gave extra urgency to his running. He could see the moonlit entrance getting nearer and nearer but could almost feel the engine breathing down his neck. He was now terrified and gritting his teeth he gave one final spurt and suddenly found himself clear of the tunnel and out into the moonlight. Without hesitating he threw himself to one side, off the track and as he rolled over in the grass, the train thundered out of the tunnel entrance.

Tom turned and looked up as he lay gasping for breath and instantly took in the sight of the engine rushing past, its whistle now echoing across the cemetery and there, standing alone on the footplate was Emily. He was horrified. The train was a runaway!

Chapter 32

Runaway Train

The train rushed headlong into the night, heading towards the junction with the cemetery line which would lead it to Brookwood station. He stood up just as the rear carriages blasted out of the tunnel, the last three now a raging inferno, bouncing back and forth with the wheels churning up the grass and mud and tearing up the sleepers. It was an amazing sight, like a train from hell hurtling through the cemetery.

Tom knew there was no time to lose. Emily was in great danger and if the train reached the main line at Brookwood station there could be a terrible accident. He knew he had to stop it. Jumping up he ran after the train but knowing he wouldn't be able to overtake it, he took a short cut across the cemetery directly towards the run-around loop which he hoped would put him in front of the engine. He ran as fast as he could, even faster than before when his life had been in danger. He was the only person now who could prevent a disaster. His breathing was becoming difficult, his chest felt as if it was on fire and he had no feeling left in his legs that were now just running mechanically. The engine was now approaching the loop but he could see with dismay that he wasn't going to reach the cab in time.

Emily was holding on in the cab and looking around in desperation, not knowing what to do but fully realising the terrible situation she was in and what would happen if the train wouldn't stop. She tried to remember what Edward had shown her and started to pull some of the levers in the hope they might do something but they seemed to make no difference and, worried that she might make things worse, she went back to the whistle to warn anyone in front. As she reached for the whistle lever she looked out the side of the cab and, in the bright moonlight, saw Tom racing towards her. At first she couldn't believe what she was seeing but quickly realised it was really him.

"Hurry Tom" she screamed instinctively but she knew he wouldn't hear her over the noise from the engine and the constant clatter of the carriages behind. Just at that moment, the last carriage broke free and rolled over into the cemetery in a cloud of sparks and flames, narrowly missing Tom. Without it the engine instantly picked up speed and Tom realised he was now falling behind and there was no chance of reaching the cab. There was only one thing left to try. He had now reached the track alongside the passing carriages and, seeing that they were rapidly pulling away from him, he reached up to one of the door handles on the carriage and grasped it. The other carriages behind were blazing furiously in the slipstream but this one was only partially on fire although he could feel the heat burning his face. The carriage was now dragging him along but he refused to let go and with a determined effort pulled himself up onto the side of the carriage. There was a running board running the full length of the carriage which served as a step for people getting in and out and he used this to walk along the side of the carriage, holding onto the door handles as he went.

When he reached the front of the carriage he realised he had to overcome his rising fear and step across a wide gap to the next carriage. Watching the track rushing past beneath him and praying that he wouldn't fall beneath the wheels, he summoned up all his courage and, reaching across to the next carriage, he made the dangerous jump landing safely. There wasn't much time left and as he struggled along the running board of the next carriage, Tom could see the station only a short distance ahead. He was surprised to see that there were men running along the track towards them. One man was standing on the track waving a red lantern but when he saw that the train wasn't going to stop he quickly leapt off and stood clear, still waving the red warning signal. As the train rushed past, George, still waving the lamp, was shocked to see his son hanging on to the side of the runaway train.

Tom had now reached the front of the first carriage but realised he couldn't get across the next gap to the engine tender. He shouted for Emily but she didn't hear him. He tried shouting louder but there was still no response. Suddenly, above all the other noise, there was an ear splitting scream that everyone could hear. It was the non-stop night mail, the fast express from Waterloo hurtling down the main line towards Brookwood at 80mph and rapidly approaching the platform. The runaway was still on the cemetery track but was now running parallel to the platform and the points leading onto the main line were now in sight. If the runaway got onto the main line and the express hit it, there would be a catastrophic disaster. The signalman had already set the cemetery line signal to *STOP* but the engine had careered through it and the white faced signalman was now standing on his balcony, frantically waving a red warning lamp.

The sound of the express whistle had frightened Emily and she rushed to the side of the engine cab to look back and see how close it was. She could see its lights in the distance, rapidly bearing down on her. Desperately she rushed to the other side of the cab to see if Tom was still running to help but, to her amazement, she saw Tom hanging on the side of the nearest carriage. The express had stopped whistling now so Tom tried shouting again. This time Emily managed to hear a few words but couldn't make out if it was Tom's voice she could hear or if it was another voice in her head. Tom was still shouting, "The long red lever. Push up the red lever." Emily turned back into the cab and seeing what she thought was the lever, she pushed it up as hard as she could. The engine responded immediately as power was removed and it began to slow but, even dragging the derailed carriages, the train still had a lot of momentum and continued forward. Without knowing how, the voice in Emily's head guided her to another small, black topped lever alongside and she instinctively rotated it to the left, immediately feeling the train braking sharply, wheels locking and screeching on the rails while sparks flew out into the darkness. The train was now rapidly slowing but the points were getting closer and closer. Emily was willing the train to stop in time and couldn't take her eyes off the fast approaching points but, just as it seemed the engine was going to run out onto the main line, it came to a standstill just a few yards from the junction in a cloud of steam and smoke. With only a few seconds to spare, the express thundered through the station and past the now stationary runaway, the express crew staring in disbelief at the burning inferno that was once a train. Emily, Tom, the signalman and the policemen in the cemetery just stopped and stared, stunned into silence as the express safely disappeared into the darkness. A major disaster had been averted.

Tom was helping Emily down from the cab as George arrived, breathless from his run back to the train and without saying anything he flung his arms around the two children and hugged them tightly as they stood there, bathed in the flickering red glow of the burning carriages.

He was shaking but eventually he simply said "Are you both all right?" Tom continued to hug his dad but Emily looked up at him and said "Please Mr Robinson, can I go home to bed now?"

Chapter 33

Aftermath

There was a lot of activity at the Necropolis cemetery the following day. Tom's parents brought him to Emily's house early that morning so they could hear the full story and by the time the children had told them of their adventure, Kate and Madge were horrified. They both gave the children a severe talking to, but their lecture was interrupted by the unannounced arrival of Mr Dawkins from London who insisted on shaking hands with Emily and Tom and thanking them for their courageous action which had averted a railway disaster.

In the end, Kate and Madge finally relented and agreed that they had both been very brave but insisted that they should never ever do anything like that again. As he finished a cup of tea, Mr Dawkins said that the Directors of the railway company would be in touch with them soon but he had to leave now to supervise the repair work to the damaged track and the removal of the wrecked carriages. He added that all funerals had been cancelled for the next few days until everything was back to normal. Emily had a special request for him, however, and when he left, she walked down the garden path with him talking quietly so no-one else could hear. Mr Dawkins listened intently and when she had finished he said "Thank you Emily, I'll see what I can do." With that he smiled, tipped his hat to her and walked off to join the repair crew waiting at the tunnel entrance.

On entering the tunnel later that morning, the first thing the repair crew found was the torn body of Sykes lying by the side of the railway track, covered in blood.

"Mmm, poor bloke" said one of them. "What a mess. Looks like he got hit by the train."

One of the other men disagreed. "Nah" he said. "I've seen people hit by trains before and they don't look like that."

The first man looked at him, doubt written on his face. "Don't be daft man, of course he got hit by the train. What else could have done that to him?"

With that they covered Sykes body and carried him outside where they rested him on a horse drawn cart. One of the porters then climbed up and drove the cart back to South Station where the body was put in the storeroom where it would wait to be examined by the police. A special train had arrived at the cemetery hauling trucks full of railway sleepers and ballast while another long truck carried new metal railway lines.

While the repair crew began work fixing the track, Mr Dawkins accompanied the foreman into the tunnel and, holding lamps above their heads, they cautiously walked through to the wide chamber. The smoke still hung heavily causing them to cough repeatedly and they were forced to hold handkerchiefs over their mouths and noses. They made a quick examination but quickly realised that there was nothing to be salvaged. The rock fall had made the whole chamber unsafe and the remains of the smashed and burned out carriages were unrecognisable. They decided that the bodies of Parker and O'Hare would have to stay buried where they were.

Mr Dawkins then walked back to another part of the wall which Emily had described to him and carefully looked around beneath some of the old fallen rocks. Then he found what he was looking for. A coffin, half buried under the rubble. He pointed to it and told the foreman that he wanted the body removed but, as it wasn't safe to dig the coffin out, the men were to just cut off the end of the wooden box and gently slide the body out. When it had been safely removed and carried to the station, the foreman was to place dynamite in the tunnel entrance and blow it up, bringing the hillside down on it so no-one could ever get in again.

Chapter 34

Epilogue

A few days later Mrs Williams arrived home bringing her husband with her. It was a very emotional homecoming and the family were left alone for a few days to give them the privacy they needed. Mr Williams was still very weak and his lungs had been damaged in the mine incident so he spent a lot of time in bed resting or just relaxing in the garden with Emily and Kate fussing around him. The doctor came most days and to the girls' great joy, he recommended that they didn't return to London as the clean, fresh air here in the country was much better for Mr Williams' breathing. Emily's parents had both been made aware of the children's little adventure by now but, despite their shock and disapproval, the matter was quickly forgotten as the family remained deliriously happy to be together again and life here at Brookwood seemed idyllic. They all decided that Mr Williams should buy *Honeysuckle Cottage* so they could continue to live here at Brookwood where everyone was so happy.

The family were also delighted to hear that Mrs Williams' art exhibition had been so successful that many of her paintings had been sold and a number of people had sent commissions for her to paint more pictures for them.

The rescue of Mr Williams from the mine was, of course, a big news event and in no time at all the newspapers were full of every aspect of the story explaining the truth about Mr Williams' experience in the mine and the criminal activities of Griffiths who was still on the run in South Africa. By far the greater story which grabbed the attention of the whole country, however, was the adventure in the cemetery and the incredible bravery of Emily and Tom who had averted a terrible train disaster. They were treated as heroes and were soon to be awarded special medals struck by the Necropolis Railway

Company together with a special payment as reward. The newspapers also revealed that a Dr Fox and one of his assistants had now been arrested at Brompton Hospital where they worked and both had now been sent for trial.

There was only one thing left to do. A week after the near disaster, a small funeral party formed up at South Station to escort Clara's coffin to her new grave. They had found where her mother and father had been buried and she was now being buried with them, all together at last. Emily was pleased for her but couldn't help shedding tears as the priest delivered his sermon at the graveside. Tom, standing beside her, said nothing but gently held her hand.

After the ceremony, as the party was making its way back to the cottage for refreshments, Emily told her mother that there was something she had to do and would it be all right if she joined them later. Her mother smiled and nodded. She was very proud of her daughter and watched her as she made her way across the cemetery towards the hill.

When Emily arrived at the ventilation shaft she wasn't surprised to find Clara sitting on the wall waiting for her.

"I thought you would come" she said, and for the first time she was smiling. "I haven't got long but I wanted to thank you for what you did for me."

Emily was pleased but shook her head saying "No, I'm here to thank you for bringing my father back to me and for saving us in the tunnel."

They looked at each other, and both recognised the special friendship they had formed.

"I can't stay" said Clara "but I want you to know that I will always remember you."

Emily could feel a lump in her throat as she asked "Will I ever see you again?"

"I don't think so" was the reply, and Clara smiled again.

Emily felt sad. "I will never forget you Clara."

Clara looked up and said "I have to go now."

Just then there was a distant screech from high above and Emily looked up. There, wheeling around in wide circles were two large birds. It was a pair of enormous buzzards slowly circling above the hill, their wings held upward in a slight "V" shape so they could catch the gentle breeze. Their motion was effortless as they glided round and round, calling loudly but never moving away from the hill. It was wonderful to watch but Emily sensed they were waiting for something. She looked back down but Clara had gone and now, sitting on the wall in front of her, was the buzzard she had become so familiar with. It put its head on one side and their eyes met one last time. Then, with one flap of its giant wings, the bird launched itself into the air and slowly flew round in a wide circle above Emily. With a few more flaps it rose higher and, catching the breeze, it quickly climbed into the air, circling all the time. Emily was fascinated and couldn't take her eyes off the scene as the bird continued to rise and finally joined the other two who were now calling more excitedly. It was a happy sight, the three birds now flying around together, soaring and diving and sometimes playfully bumping into each other. As they circled they continued to rise higher and higher, getting smaller all the time until eventually Emily lost sight of them in the clouds. Emily continued to watch in silence for several minutes before whispering "Goodbye Clara" and, with a tear in her eye, she turned and walked home.

Printed in Great Britain
by Amazon